ROSIE SWANSON:
Fourth-Grade Geek
for President

☆

BARBARA PARK

ALFRED A. KNOPF, NEW YORK

To the special man I get to call my dad . . .
Happy eighty-fifth birthday!

— B. P.

THIS IS A BORZOI BOOK
PUBLISHED BY ALFRED A. KNOPF, INC.

Text copyright © 1991 by Barbara Park
Jacket art copyright © 1991 by Eric Peterson
All rights reserved under International and
Pan-American Copyright Conventions.
Published in the United States by
Alfred A. Knopf, Inc., New York, and
simultaneously in Canada by Random House
of Canada Limited, Toronto. Distributed by
Random House, Inc., New York.

Book design by Mina Greenstein
Manufactured in the United States of America
2   4   6   8   10   9   7   5   3   1

Library of Congress Cataloging-in-Publication Data
Park, Barbara. Rosie Swanson : fourth-grade geek for
president / by Barbara Park. p.   cm. Summary: Just
average Rosie runs for class president against two of
the most popular kids in the fourth grade.
ISBN 0-679-82094-9 (trade)
ISBN 0-679-92094-3 (lib. bdg.)
[1. Elections—Fiction.   2. Popularity—Fiction.
3. Schools—Fiction.]   I. Title.   PZ7.P2197Ro
1991 [Fic]—dc20   91-8616

ROSIE SWANSON:
Fourth-Grade Geek
for President

Rosie Swanson—
Secret Informer

"HEY! YOU! NERDHEADS!
GET OFF THE SWINGS!"

The voice came from behind us.

Quickly, Maxie and Earl and I spun around.
Three giant sixth-grade boys were hurrying
toward us.

"YOU THREE! THE FAT KID, THE
SKINNY KID, AND THE FOUR-EYES!
SOMETHING WRONG WITH YOUR EARS,
DUDES? WE SAID, GET OFF THE SWINGS!
IT'S OUR TURN."

Earl jumped right up. Since he's a little on
the plumpish side, he always likes to get a
head start.

I hunched over and tried to pull my head
inside my sweater. Everything fit except my
glasses.

"No, wait, Earl! Don't run," I ordered
through my buttons. "If you run they might

chase you. Let's just pretend we didn't hear them."

Earl sat back down. Even though he and Maxie are in fifth grade and I'm only in fourth, they still listen to me sometimes.

Maxie's eyes were squeezed shut. "I'm a dead person," he muttered fearfully. He started to spell it. "D-E-A-D P-E-R-S—"

"No you're not," I interrupted. "We're not going to die. Who ever heard of dying on a swing set?"

Maxie looked over at me and frowned. "I've got news for you. Little people die wherever big people kill them. It's a law of physics. Look it up."

The sixth-graders were right behind us now. Angry that we hadn't moved, they grabbed the chains of our swings and began shaking them.

"You guys don't hear too good, do you?" said the one in the baggy pants.

Earl started to whimper. I felt like whimpering too. But something inside me just wouldn't let me give him my swing.

"We were here first," I managed.

The three bullies laughed. *"We were here first, we were here first,"* they mimicked in baby voices.

Then they all walked over to where I was

sitting and stuck their heads right in my face. "GET OFF, GIRLIE!" they roared.

I don't liked to be shouted at. Also, I don't like being called girlie.

"These are our swings too," I told them.

Hearing myself say that gave me a little more courage. I sat up straighter. "And guess what else? If you don't leave us alone, I'm going to run right to the office and report you to the principal."

Baggy Pants jerked my swing so hard I thought my head would snap off.

"Gee, girlie. I'm shaking in my shoes," he said. "Aren't you, Frankie? Aren't you shaking in your shoes?"

After that, they began twisting our chains around and around and around till our swings were all wound up in little knots and we were way off the ground.

"We don't care that you're doing this, you know," I spouted. "We like this. This is fun. We love being twisted around."

The bullies stopped winding our chains.

"ONE . . . TWO . . . THREE!" they hollered together.

On "three," they grabbed our swing seats and spun us around as hard as they could.

"Bye-bye, you little dipsticks!" they called as they ran off.

5

I've never twirled so fast in my life. Not even on that carnival ride where everyone throws up.

Next to me, Earl was making a high-pitched whining sound—like a siren, sort of. Earl is the wheezy type, so strange sounds are pretty normal for him. He keeps squeezy nose drops in his pocket to clear out his sinuses and junk. Also, he has a mouth inhaler. It wasn't much help to him now, though. Not when he was spinning out of control.

Maxie said a bad word. It was only one syllable, but he dragged it out for the entire time he was spinning.

It took forever for us to unwind. I mean it. It seemed like we would spin for years. But even after our swings stopped, none of us got up right away. We just laid our heads on our knees and kind of moaned for a while until the world stopped moving around so fast.

Finally, I held on to the chains and stood up. Slowly letting go, I tried to smooth out my dress without falling over.

"I don't care," I said, trying to sound confident. "We did the right thing. Bullies like that make me sick. They don't own the school, you know. Sometimes kids like us just have to stand up for our rights. You know

6

. . . just like we did today. Right, you guys? Am I right?"

Maxie raised his head. His eyes looked like cartoon eyes—very round and white with a little brown dot in the middle.

Earl was holding his hand over his mouth.

"Okay. I *know* it wasn't fun. But at least we didn't give in. We're just as much a part of this school as anybody else. And it's time we acted like it."

Slowly, Maxie got off the swing and helped Earl stand up.

"Well, isn't it?" I asked them again. "Isn't it time that we acted like we're part of this school?"

They both fell over in the grass. I still can't believe I'm best friends with these two. But I am.

"Come on, you guys," I said. "We need to go report those creeps to the principal's office before the bell rings."

Earl shook his head wildly. "Oh no! No way! Not me! Forget it. I'm *never* going back to Mr. Shivers' office! Not ever! I still get nightmares about the last time we met. I mean *real* nightmares. The kind where I wake up all tangled in the sheets and I have to turn on the light."

"I agree," said Maxie. "We'd have to be crazy to go back to the principal's office. If Mr. Shivers gets to know the three of us any better, we'll be on his Christmas list."

I just sighed. I hated to admit it, but they were right. It wasn't even November yet, and each of us had been sent to the office two times already. Actually, it's where we first met.

I was sent for passing notes. I wasn't passing them to other kids, though. I was passing them to my teacher, Mr. Jolly. That's because I'm Rosie Swanson—Secret Informer. Reporting on my fellow classmates is my job.

Maxie and Earl don't know I'm a secret informer. I mean, they know I'm a nut about following rules and everything. Like I always make them cross at the crosswalks and stuff. But I've never told them about the note writing. I'm afraid they'd think I'm a tattletale. And I'm not.

Secret informers are different from tattletales. We don't tell on kids just to get them in trouble. We do it for their own good. And also for the good of the world community.

I've been a secret informer since the summer I turned seven. That's the summer my mother and I went into a candy store at the beach and I spotted an old lady stealing a piece of saltwater taffy. She took it out of one of the jars, unwrapped it, and popped it right into her mouth without paying for it.

I couldn't believe it! I'm talking about a grandma here! Except for when they drive, you almost never see grandmas break the law.

So I stopped what I was doing and watched her chew. Only instead of being embarrassed, she winked at me. You know . . . like we were both in on this together.

I've thought about it a lot since then. And I think winking was the meanest thing that old woman could have done. 'Cause she tried to make a little girl think it was okay to steal candy. And that was wrong, you know? It just was.

I still get angry about it. Since then, I've taught myself to say "The old lady took a taffy" without moving my lips, but I doubt that I'll ever get to use it.

Anyway, after that summer I decided that I was never going to just stand around while somebody broke the law again. That's when I became a secret informer.

I've had a lot of success with my notes over the years. Take Ronald Milligan, for instance. Because of me, Ronald has stopped blowing his nose in the drinking fountain. I take a lot of pride in that.

But this year my teacher, Mr. Jolly, hasn't really appreciated my help very much. That's why he sent me to the principal's office. And like I said before, that's where I met Maxie and Earl.

"I wish I ran this school," Earl grumbled as he unwrapped a brand-new package of Rolaids. In addition to his other problems, Earl Wilber has what you'd call a nervous stomach.

"If I ran this school, I'd lock creeps like that in a dark, smelly dungeon," he said. "Then I'd hire this really mean guy—like the Joker or somebody—to go in and make fun of them until they cried."

Maxie smiled sympathetically. "Forget about it, Earl," he said. "You can't let farkleberries like that get to you."

Farkleberry is one of Maxie's special words. Finding weird words in the dictionary is sort of a hobby of his. That's because he's a giant brain.

Maxie's very different from Earl and me. But even though the three of us aren't anything alike, if you put us all together we'd make a pretty well-rounded person. That's important, I think.

Earl was still growling. "Yeah, well, I still

wish I could run the school. They're having those stupid class elections in a few weeks, and the same popular kids will get elected who *always* get elected. And not one of them knows anything about how it feels to be called names and pushed around."

"Run," Maxie said simply.

Earl's face went funny. "Oh geez! Not again!" he cried. Then he took off running.

Maxie rolled his eyes. "No, Earl," he called. "I mean *run*. Run for office."

Earl came strolling back. He was trying to act casual, but you could tell he was a little bit embarrassed. "Yeah, right. Me . . . president of the fifth grade," he said. "Very funny, Mr. Funnyperson. That's so funny I forgot to laugh."

Maxie shrugged. "Well, you're always complaining about the creeps around here, aren't you? So maybe if you ran for president of the fifth grade, you could change some stuff."

I thought about what he was saying for a second. It's funny, but the idea that one of *us* could run for class office had just never occurred to me before.

"What about me?" I asked boldly. "I bet I'd make a pretty good *fourth*-grade president, don't you think? Huh, you guys? Don't you think I'd be good?"

Maxie and Earl didn't answer. They just gave each other one of those looks.

"Hey! Why did you do that? What's wrong with me being president of the fourth grade?"

"Nothing," replied Earl. "Nothing's exactly *wrong* with it. It's just that sometimes you can be a little bit . . . well, you know . . ."

"Bossy and overbearing," Max blurted out.

"I am not!" I snapped. "I'm not bossy and whatever that other word means. I just happen to believe in following the rules, that's all. What's so wrong with that? In case you've forgotten, my grandfather happens to be a retired police detective."

Maxie's mouth dropped open. "No! Really? You're kidding! Gee, I think that's only the jillionth time you've told us that. Isn't it, Earl? Isn't that the jillionth?"

Earl pretended to count on his fingers. Then he shook his head no. "Jillionth and one," he corrected.

They were only teasing, but it still sort of hurt my feelings. I'm very proud of my grandfather. He's part of the reason I'm such a good citizen.

He and my mother and I all live in the same

12

house that Mom grew up in. It's just the three of us. We're our own kind of family. We would have been a regular kind of family, only my father and my grandmom both died when I was a baby.

I don't have any brothers or sisters. I used to have a girlfriend who was *almost* like a sister. But we haven't spoken in over a year. That's when she spray-painted a bad word on the sidewalk and I had to report her to the police.

Granddad still hangs around the station a lot. Sometimes I go down there with him and we have a soda and this one sergeant lets me wear his hat. I've met criminals before, too. Not the real dangerous kind. But still, most of them haven't shaved for a while.

"It's not very nice calling me bossy, you know," I said at last. "And anyway, I don't care what you say, I still think I'd make a good class president. I have excellent values and I follow the rules. And I also have a bullhorn which I could bring to school to boss kids around with."

Maxie raised his eyebrows. I knew this would impress him.

"Seriously? You have an actual bullhorn? A *real* one? Like the kind on TV?"

"Yes," I said proudly. "It's my grandfather's, but I've used it before. Just ask my mother if you don't believe me. Last summer I snuck it outside and made her come out of the house with her hands up. I told her I had the place surrounded."

Earl was even more impressed than Maxie. "She did that? She came out with her hands up?"

"Well, sort of. I mean, at first she just went to the window and shook her fist at me. But then a small crowd began to gather in our front yard. And they started chanting, 'Come out, Helen. Come out.' And so finally she ran outside and snatched the bullhorn away from me."

"Wow," said Earl.

"Yeah, wow," I agreed.

I didn't tell him the best part, though. That's because I didn't know exactly how to put it. But the best part about that bullhorn was what it did to my voice. 'Cause a bullhorn automatically turns a little voice like mine into a loud, booming voice. A voice that everybody stops to listen to.

And that's important, you know? To be listened to, I mean.

Seriously, it makes you feel bigger than anything.

To Run or Not to Run?

☆

ROSEBUD SWANSON FOR PRESIDENT OF THE
FOURTH GRADE.

The idea just kept flashing on and off in my head like a neon sign. I'm not kidding. Ever since I mentioned it on the playground, I just couldn't get it out of my mind.

ROSEBUD SWANSON FOR PRESIDENT OF THE
FOURTH GRADE.

Boy. That'd show everyone, wouldn't it? I bet if I was president of the whole entire fourth grade, Maxie and Earl and I would *never* get picked on again.

The idea wasn't totally impossible, you know. I mean, you don't *have* to be cute or popular to run for president. It's not an actual *requirement* or anything.

At school we have a poster of the Presidents of the United States, and practically *none* of those guys were cute. George Washington even wore a stupid-looking wig. I realize that wigs were in style back then, but I still think one of his friends should have pulled him over and said, "George. The wig. Lose it."

Anyway, I guess it was a coincidence, but while all these thoughts were floating around in my head Mr. Jolly made an announcement about the class election.

"There's going to be a candidates' meeting for fourth-graders right after school," he told us. "Anyone who is interested in running for class office should report to room thirteen— that's Mrs. Munson's room—at three o'clock sharp."

As soon as he said it, I got butterflies in my stomach. Chills, too. The kind of chills that don't go away when you rub them.

I raised my hand. "That's today, right, sir?" I called out. "The meeting's today?"

A couple of kids turned around and looked at me. Then they sort of rolled their eyes. You know . . . like they couldn't believe a person like me would even *think* about running.

Judith Topper, the jerky girl who sits right in front of me, did the same thing.

"Yeah, right, Rosie," she said. "Like *you* could really win an election. Have you looked in the mirror lately? You're nobody."

"Oh really, Judith Stupid-head?" I snapped. "Well, if I'm nobody, then who are you talking to, huh? Are you just talking to the air, Judith Stupid-head?"

Judith made a face. "Geek," she said. Then she turned back around.

That's when I really started to boil. It's just not fair, that's all. Why does being cute and popular *always* have to be so important? Why isn't it ever enough just to be nice and average? You know, just a regular person.

There're lots of us around, you know. In fact, almost everybody in my entire class is just a regular person. Some of them even wear glasses like I do.

Also, there are crooked teeth and braces and dumb haircuts and big noses and ears that stick out. We even have two boys in our room who can put you to sleep just by talking to you.

I felt myself relax a little. *Average.* It's not a bad word, really. It's nice, in fact. Comfortable, sort of.

Norman Beeman caught me looking at him and blushed. Norman is one of the dumb haircuts. Also, he has fat freckled fingers and he wears fishing boots to school on Fridays. I don't know why. I would like to ask him, but Norman Beeman scares me.

He'd probably vote for me, though. Norman Beeman would probably love to vote for a person who wasn't perfect or popular. I bet a lot of kids would.

The more I thought about it, the better I felt about my chances. I mean, I was still really nervous about going to the meeting and all. But part of me was starting to get excited again.

During geography, I even closed my eyes and imagined myself giving my victory speech. I was standing on the school stage with my bullhorn. And there was this giant American flag behind me. And I was thanking all the "average kids" who voted for me. And then I thanked the "below-average ones," too. After that, I found Judith Topper in the crowd and had the police drag her out of the media center and beat her up.

Three o'clock came fast that day. When the bell rang, my heart was pounding faster than ever. I picked up my stuff and ran straight to the girls' bathroom. Because when you're nervous about a meeting, the worst thing you can do is be the first one there.

I washed my hands for a while. If you dry each finger with a separate paper towel, you can really use up a lot of time. I would have been there longer, but Mrs. Galonka, the head custodian, came in, saw all the towels I was using, and started yelling, "Whoa, whoa, whoa!"

I left the girls' room and walked as slowly as I could to room 13. Then I took a deep breath and went inside.

Mrs. Munson and Mr. Jolly were standing in the front of the room. There are four fourth-grade teachers at Dooley Elementary. But since Mr. Jolly and Mrs. Munson have been there the longest, they're almost always the bosses.

Mr. Jolly smiled at me. "Rosie Swanson. Great! I was beginning to think that no one from my class was going to show."

Mrs. Munson went to the door and looked up and down the hall. "Any more stragglers?" she asked.

I didn't appreciate being called a straggler, but I didn't say anything. I just went straight to the back of the room and sat down. The other kids were sitting nearer the front. I knew almost all of them.

Nic and Vic Timmerman were right in front of Mrs. Munson's desk. In case you haven't

19

guessed it, Nic and Vic are twins. The weird kind. The kind who don't exactly understand that they're two separate people. Like if you call one of them, they both come. In first grade, when Nic broke his wrist, Vic wore a sling. Also, they finish each other's sentences, just like Huey, Dewey, and Louie.

One seat over from the Timmerman twins was this really cute girl named Summer Lynne Jones. That's her real name, too. Summer Lynne. It must be nice to have a mother who doesn't feel it's necessary to name you after her dead aunt Rosebud.

Two desks behind Summer Lynne Jones was this boy I went to kindergarten with. His name is Alan Allen. I would like to make fun of it, but I have an uncle named Harry Harry. And anyway, when you're the best soccer player in the fourth grade, and you look almost exactly like Michael Jordan, your name could be Piggly Wiggly and no one would care. They'd just pat you on the back, say, "Good game, Piggly," and that would be that.

Sitting next to the window was Louise the Disease. That's not her real name, but she always has a cold, so that's what everyone calls her. She deliberately sneezed on me in assembly last year. I reported her to the nurse, but no action was taken.

Roxanne Handleman was right behind Louise the Disease. I used to know Roxanne, but I don't anymore. One time when we were in kindergarten, she came over to my house to play. She wore a nurse's outfit and made me call her Florence. It was the longest afternoon of my life.

Next to her was this girl named Karla something who I didn't know much about. Then there were three kids from Mrs. Munson's class. I didn't know them, either, but they were acting really cool, so I decided not to like them.

Mr. Jolly grabbed a piece of chalk and walked over to the board. "Okay, let's get started. I want to welcome you to our meeting this afternoon and tell you how glad Mrs. Munson and I are that so many of you have decided to run for class office."

Then he took his chalk and wrote the words "President, Vice President, Secretary, and Treasurer." Underneath each title he left room for names.

"The first thing we have to do is find out which office each of you wants to run for," he said. "So let's begin with president. How many of you came here today to run for president of the fourth grade? Let's see your hands."

My heart started to pound again. I closed my eyes and secretly prayed that I would be the only one. When I opened them again, Nic and Vic Timmerman were waving their hands like crazy.

Mr. Jolly seemed puzzled. "Wait a second here . . . you mean, you *both* want to run for president? Do you really think that's a good idea, guys? For two brothers to run *against* each other?"

The Timmerman twins shook their heads. "We don't want to run *against* each other, Mr. Jolly," said Vic. "We want to run *together*. You know, two presidents—"

"—for the price of one," finished Nic excitedly.

Mrs. Munson didn't waste a second. "No way," she said flatly. "Absolutely not. No way, gentlemen."

Nic and Vic looked shocked. "Why?" asked Vic. "How come?" asked Nic. "It'd be perfect. We could do twice as much work as one president could. And if one of us got sick, the other one could—"

"—take his place," finished Vic. "It'd be—"

"—perfect," said Nic.

Mrs. Munson tapped her foot on the floor. 22 "I'm sorry, boys, but life is not a Heckle and Jeckle cartoon. We're trying to teach you something about government. And in *our* government, there's only *one* president. So why don't you two think it over, and we'll come back to you in a few minutes."

The Timmermans didn't answer. They put their heads down on their desks and started to sulk.

Mrs. Munson moved along. "Okay . . . anybody else for president?" she wanted to know.

I took a deep breath and started to raise my hand in the air. That's when Alan Allen suddenly called out, "Me! I do!"

Then Summer Lynne Jones raised her hand too. She fluttered her fingers and waved to get Mr. Jolly's attention.

My insides went limp. I mean it. It was like somebody let all my air out or something. I should have known this would happen. The popular kids *always* run for president. And they always win, too.

With those two running against me, I wouldn't stand a chance. Why would anyone vote for nice and average *me,* when they could vote for cute and popular *them*?

Mr. Jolly searched the room for more volunteers. I sat on my hands and slumped as low as I could in my seat.

Finally, he moved on. "Okay then. How

23

about vice president? Who came here today to run for VP?"

Both of the girls from Mrs. Munson's room called out their names. Then they looked at each other and crossed their fingers. I wondered if they would still be so buddy-buddy after the election.

When Mr. Jolly got to secretary, Karla something and Roxanne Handleman both started waving. Roxanne tried to raise her hand the highest. Seeing this, Karla something got on her knees and stretched even taller. Finally, Roxanne stood on her chair.

Watching them made me embarrassed to be a girl.

Next came treasurer. Louise the Disease raised her Kleenex over her head. "Louise Marie Smythe!" she declared loudly.

Then the boy from Mrs. Munson's class cupped his hands around his mouth and shouted, "Robert Moneypenny! Robert Moneypenny for treasurer!"

Louise the Disease's smile faded. She stared at him in disbelief.

"That's your name? Your name is Robert Moneypenny?"

The boy smiled smugly and leaned his chair back on two legs.

Louise the Disease put her hands on her hips. "That's not fair," she called. "Is that fair? You can't have a name like that, can you?"

Mrs. Munson said it was fair. Louise the Disease turned to Robert Moneypenny and coughed on him.

After that, there were only three of us left. Nic and Vic and me.

Mr. Jolly went back to the twins. "Have you gentlemen decided what you want to do yet?"

Nic and Vic looked at each other and began raising their eyebrows up and down. It was really creepy.

Finally, they looked up. "Treasurer and vice president," they announced unenthusiastically.

Mr. Jolly picked up his chalk. "Okay. Good. Which one wants which job?"

Nic shrugged glumly. "What difference—"

"—does it make?" said Vic.

Meanwhile, Mrs. Munson was looking in my direction. She pointed. "Okay, back there. How 'bout you? We need to know what office you're planning to run for. We've got lots of other things to discuss and we're running out of time."

Everyone turned around. That's the only bad

thing about sitting in the back. Everybody always turns around.

I gritted my teeth. I didn't know what to do. I mean, I've never been a quitter before. But . . .

"Rosie?" urged Mr. Jolly. "Come on. We need to know."

I closed my eyes and bit my bottom lip. "President," I said at last. "I guess I'm running for president."

Me and Thomas Jefferson

☆

It was Saturday. And as usual, Maxie and Earl and I were hanging out in Maxie's garage. Maxie's father has this old 1955 red and white Chevy that the three of us sort of use as a clubhouse. Mr. Zuckerman thinks that he's going to fix it up someday. But Maxie says it'll just rust in the garage for another twenty years, and then some old man with overalls and no teeth will come haul it to the dump for fifty bucks.

Anyhow, we were in the car having this discussion about whether dogs were better than cats. But since I was still depressed about the election meeting, I was mostly just pouting. I don't really believe in pretending to be happy when you're not. Mostly I believe that you should burden your friends with your problems.

Besides, the conversation was turning so stupid it was embarrassing. Earl said that stinky cats needed stinky litter boxes. And then Maxie said that putrid dogs drank from putrid toilets. And finally Earl got mad and shouted, "Oh yeah? Well, I'd rather drink out of a putrid toilet any old day than use a stinky litter box!"

I looked at them both with disgust and turned my head toward the window. "Well, guess what?" I muttered glumly. "I don't know and I don't care."

Maxie and Earl sighed. Until then, they had been trying to ignore my bad mood. But I could have told them it wouldn't work.

"Okay, okay, okay," Maxie said. "I guess we might as well get this over with. What the heck's the matter with you this morning, anyway? Why are you acting like such a dingle?"

"I am not a dingle," I retorted. "It just so happens that I have a lot on my mind. And don't ask me what it is, either. Because I don't feel like talking about it."

They didn't ask. I waited, but they didn't. That's the trouble with boys. When you tell them not to ask, they don't.

"Well, okay," I said at last. "I'll tell you.

But when I'm finished telling you, I don't want to talk about it."

Then I took a deep breath. "I'm running for president of the fourth grade."

Maxie's mouth dropped open. "Whaaaat?"

Earl's eyes got very wide. "You're kidding!"

"No. I'm not kidding. And I don't want to talk about it, because it makes me feel pukey inside."

Earl rolled down the windows to let in some fresh air. He takes "pukey" very seriously.

"I'm not really going to puke, Earl. If I was going to puke, I would have done it by now. You should hear who I'm running against, though. It'll make *you* sick."

"Who?" they asked.

I squeezed my eyes shut and swallowed hard. "Summer Lynne Jones and Alan Allen, that's who."

Then I waited again. You know . . . waited for them to say something to make me feel better. Something about how Summer Lynne Jones and Alan Allen were no big deal and I had nothing to worry about.

But when I finally opened my eyes, they both seemed to be in shock. Earl had covered his face with his hands, like he had just seen a slasher movie. And Maxie's stupid mouth had dropped open again. "Ho boy," he muttered under his breath.

Finally, Earl leaned over and gave me a sympathetic pat. "Tough break," he said. "I know exactly how you feel."

For some reason, this really annoyed me. People are always saying they know exactly how you feel, when they don't know exactly how you feel at all.

"How, Earl?" I asked him. "How do you know exactly how I feel? Have you ever run for president of your class against two of the most popular kids in the school?"

"No," he admitted. "But I came very close to being in an election one time. In second grade, I got up the nerve to nominate myself for Cub of the Month. Only as soon as I said it, the den mother jumped right off the couch and started shouting, 'Get real, Earl! Get real!' "

He paused a second and shook his head sadly. "I *still* can't believe that woman did that."

Maxie couldn't believe it, either. "You told your mother, of course. I *hope* you told your mother."

Earl looked down at his lap and stared at his hands awhile. Finally, he sighed. "The den mother *was* my mother," he said quietly.

Maxie just looked at him a minute. Then he totally cracked up. I mean it. He doubled up into a little ball and started rolling all around the front seat.

"Not funny! Not funny!" yelled Earl. But that only made Maxie laugh harder.

Suddenly, I just wanted to go home. I reached for the door handle. But as I did Maxie's head appeared over the top of the seat. He had tears in his eyes from laughing so hard.

"Hey! Wait! Where're you goin'?" he asked, trying to get himself under control. "You're not leaving, are you? Come on, Rosie. Don't go. We've got a lot to talk about."

One of my feet was already on the floor of the garage. In a flash, Maxie jumped out of the car, put my foot back inside, and hopped back in the front seat.

"Listen to me!" he insisted. "It's *good* that you're running in this election! It's not as hopeless as you think. *You're* the one who's always talking about how we should stand up for ourselves. So *do* it! I can help you win! I *know* I can. My father ran for town council last year, so I know a ton about campaigning."

That didn't really surprise me. Maxie knows a ton about everything.

"Did your dad win?" asked Earl.

Maxie frowned. "What does that have to do with anything, Earl? There are more important things in life than just winning, you know. Winning, winning, winning—that's all anyone ever thinks about."

Earl turned to me. "He didn't win," he mouthed softly.

"So what?" Maxie retorted. "He could have. The only reason he lost was that this giant fardel named Leona Tisdale went knocking on people's doors at all hours of the night begging for votes."

He frowned again. "Leona was a woman with no pride."

Then he paused and added, "And one of those really big flashlights."

I reached for the door again.

"No, Rosie. Stay. I *know* I can help you. I'm serious."

More than anything, I wanted to believe him.

I took my hand off the door. "How?"

Maxie smiled confidently. "Trust me. All you need to win an election is a smart campaign manager and a good platform."

I stared at him blankly. A good platform? What the heck was *that*? What was he talking about now?

"Have you thought about it yet?" he continued. "Your campaign platform, I mean."

Desperately trying to think of what to say, I let my eyes drift around the car.

"Oh yeah?" I said finally. "Well, guess what, Mr. Smartie Pants? I don't even know what a campaign platform is. So there."

Maxie just shrugged. "So what? It's simple. A campaign platform is just a set of issues that are important to you. Each issue is called a plank. And all the planks put together make up the platform. You know, like boards make a floor, sort of. The planks of the platform are the things you want to do if you get elected, like . . . like—"

"A dungeon plank," interrupted Earl excitedly. "Remember that, Rosie? We talked about it the other day! You could promise to put all the creeps of the school in a dungeon where they can't bother the rest of us. It doesn't have to be a real dungeon or anything. Just a big, dark, smelly room with no ventilation. Like the cafeteria."

Maxie groaned. "Earl, we're trying to be serious here."

Earl nodded. "All right, okay . . . forget the dungeon. How 'bout a hole? We'll just dig about a ten-foot hole in the corner of the playground, and when a kid does something mean, we'll lower him down there for a few minutes—"

He paused. "—with a snake—"

"Earrlll," growled Max.

"—or a small crocodile, perhaps."

That did it. Maxie leaped over the seat and pounced right on top of him. Then the two of them fell on the floor and began wrestling all over the place. I had to get out of the car to protect myself.

Some of the time they were laughing. The rest of the time Maxie was yelling, "Ow! That hurts! Knock it off!"

Finally, Earl let him up.

Maxie's face was bright pink and he had little red blotches all over his arms. Also, his clothes were twisted and wrinkled and one of his shoes and socks had come off.

He got back in the front seat again. Then he took a deep breath, dusted off, and quietly muttered the same thing he always does after he gets pounded.

"I won."

Earl just smiled.

"This isn't helping, you know," I grumbled, getting back in the car. "Neither one of

you is being helpful at all. Why do I even need

a campaign platform, anyway? Why can't I just hang up a bunch of posters that say ROSIE SWANSON FOR PRESIDENT like everyone else does? No one else ever has a stupid *platform*."

Maxie didn't answer for a minute, but I could tell there was something on his mind.

"I don't know exactly how to say this, Rosie," he replied at last. "But just think about it. You're going to be running against the two most popular kids in the fourth grade. One of them is a star soccer player, and the other one looks like a model. If all you do is hang up a few posters, who do you think is going to win?"

I didn't *have* to think about it. I just hid my face behind my hands and moaned.

"Stop it," he ordered. "Listen to what I'm saying. If you have a good campaign and you give kids a good reason to vote for you, you don't have to be a great athlete or a beauty queen to win an election."

Earl nodded in agreement. "I think he's right, Rosie. I did a report on Thomas Jefferson once, and he had the biggest nostrils I've ever seen. I mean it. The man could fit an ear of corn up his nose."

I uncovered my face and stared at him a

moment. "Thank you, Earl. I feel much better now."

Maxie wouldn't give up. "Come on, Rosie. Earl and I will help you. We'll work on your campaign platform together. With all three of us thinking, we're bound to come up with some great ideas. You know what they say—three heads are better than one. Right?"

I looked over at Earl. He was measuring his nostrils.

I just sighed.

Thank You,
Norman Beeman

I don't pout forever. Mostly just two or three days at a time. Once, I pouted for over a week and a half, but that was pretty unusual. The red light was out at the end of my street, and my mother refused to let me direct traffic.

Anyway, after I got home that day, I curled up in my grandfather's big easy chair and thought about what Maxie had said. You know, about how all I needed to win the election was a smart campaign manager and a good platform.

Then I closed my eyes. And before I knew it, I was imagining myself on the school stage again. And that same American flag was draped behind me, and the crowd was cheering my victory. And I bowed. And the gold crown I was wearing fell off my head.

I smiled. I realize that the president of fourth grade doesn't really get to wear a gold crown, but it still looked very attractive on me.

By the time the candidates met again on Monday morning, I was feeling a little more positive about things. The meeting was called so that Mr. Jolly and Mrs. Munson could tell us more about how to run our campaigns. It didn't take long. Mostly they just told us about making campaign buttons and posters and junk. They said that there was no limit on the number of posters you could make but they had to be in good taste. Good taste means no blood or cuss words.

Also, they told us that there were ninety-five kids in the fourth grade (forty-four boys and fifty-one girls), so that's how many campaign buttons we should make.

The whole time they were talking, Louise the Disease was sitting in the middle of the room with this real annoyed expression on her face. It looked like she was about to blow up or something. She practically did, too. As soon as Mr. Jolly stopped talking, Louise shot right out of her chair.

"Could someone please tell Robert Moneypenny he's not allowed to pass out real money," she blurted out. "He says his campaign buttons are going to be pennies, but that's not allowed, is it?"

Then she pointed her finger in his face. "You can't pass out real money, Robert. That's just like buying votes. And in this country you're not allowed to buy votes. This is America, mister."

Mr. Jolly turned his back to the group. I'm pretty sure he was trying not to laugh. Meanwhile, Mrs. Munson informed Robert that he'd have to use fake pennies, instead of real ones.

"Seeee? Told ja," said Louise the Disease happily.

After that, Mr. Jolly went on to explain more about the election. "In addition to making your campaign posters and buttons, there will be two meetings with the entire fourth grade. The first meeting will be held next week. It will be called 'Meet the Candidates,' and you will introduce yourselves to the class and talk a little bit about your campaigns. Directly after the first meeting, you will be given time to start hanging your posters."

Mr. Jolly looked down at his notes. "The second meeting will be on Election Day. That's the day some of you will give your campaign speeches. As it gets closer to the election, Mrs. Munson and I will be available to help you with your thoughts."

"Questions?" asked Mrs. Munson, looking at the clock which was just about to ring. "Make them quick."

Summer Lynne Jones raised her hand. "Is it okay if our friends help us make our posters? I mean, we don't have to do it all by ourselves, do we? I was thinking about having a poster party and inviting a bunch of kids over to help me."

Mr. Jolly nodded enthusiastically. "Great. That's a good idea. The more kids that we can involve in this election, the better."

"How 'bout my soccer team?" asked Alan Allen. "Even though some of them don't go to this school, can I still use a poster with them in it? I've got this really awesome picture where they're carrying me around on their shoulders at the last game. It was in the newspaper. Maybe you saw it."

Mr. Jolly smiled. "I didn't see it, Alan. But go ahead and use it if you want to."

"Are you allowed to vote for yourself?" asked Roxanne Handleman.

Mrs. Munson seemed surprised. "Yes, of course you can. If you think you're the best candidate, certainly you can vote for yourself."

"How many times?" I called.

Everybody laughed.

It wasn't a joke.

For the rest of the day, the election was all I could think about. I couldn't concentrate on my schoolwork at all. When Judith Topper turned around to sneak a peek at my math, I didn't even have anything for her to copy.

Maxie was right. Unless I could give everyone a good reason to vote for me, I wouldn't stand a chance. I'd never be able to compete with a poster like Alan Allen's. And I sure didn't have enough friends to have a poster party.

But still, I didn't want to quit. Quitting has just never seemed right to me. It would have meant giving up my dream of ever being on top. And anyway, I could still sort of picture that gold crown on my head.

Think, Rosie! I ordered, staring blankly into my math book. *Think of a way to get some votes!* But no matter how hard I tried, I couldn't come up with anything that sounded good enough.

I mean, there were lots of things I could think of to make the school a nicer place. Like I've always thought it should be illegal to have **41** milk come out your nose at the lunch table.

But I didn't think that would win an election for me.

Anyway, I was just sort of letting my mind wander, when I happened to glance over at Norman Beeman. Something was wrong. *Really* wrong. He was all doubled over, and his face looked greener than usual.

At first I thought he was searching for something on the floor. But then he started hugging his stomach and going "Ooooooo ooooooo." So I knew what was going to happen next.

Ruthie Firestone knew too. She tried to make a getaway. But she was only a step or two down the aisle, when Norman's lunch came up all over the place. Including the back of Ruthie Firestone's left leg.

I won't go into all the details of what followed, except to say that Ruthie Firestone went off the deep end and ran around the room screaming, "GET IT OFF ME! GET IT OFF ME!"

Norman handled the situation pretty coolly, I think. He went to the boys' room, splashed a little water on his face, and was back in time to watch Mr. Jim, the custodian, clean up.

42   "You the one who did this?" I heard Mr. Jim mutter disgustedly.

Norman nodded. "Salisbury steak and peas," he said calmly. "What choice did I have?"

Anyway, the really weird part about all of it was that Norman Beeman saved the day for me. I mean it. By the time school was over, I knew exactly what my campaign platform would be.

"I've got it!" I hollered, as soon as I saw Maxie and Earl on the playground. "I've got it! I've got it! I've got it!"

"Got what?" asked Maxie.

Before I answered, I looked around. When you've got an idea as great as mine, you can't go blabbing it out for the whole world to hear. I lowered my voice to a whisper.

"The perfect campaign platform, that's what," I answered. "Wait'll you hear it. Just wait'll you hear it."

I made them wait until we got all the way to my house. I don't know how I held it in that long. It's a miracle I didn't start to swell up or something.

"A hint. I'll give you a hint," I teased as I closed my front door safely behind me. "Today during math, Norman Beeman tossed his turnips."

Earl covered his mouth with his hand. Maxie just looked puzzled.

"Okay. Hint number two: He'd eaten a hot lunch from the cafeteria."

Still, Maxie just shrugged and shook his head. "I don't know. I give up."

"Cafeteria food!" I yelled excitedly. "Cafeteria food, Max! Just think about it! It's perfect!"

Earl frowned. "Cafeteria food is perfect? Are you nuts? Last week my mother made me buy the Alpo platter. It was some kind of slimy meat, with brown-looking jelly gunk on top."

He shivered and pulled out his pack of Rolaids.

I clapped my hands together. "Don't you get it, Earl? That's why it's so perfect! It's gross! The cafeteria food is gross, and I'm going to try and change it! That's why kids will vote for me. 'Cause everybody hates the lunches, and I'm the candidate who's going to do something about it!"

I put my arm around Earl's shoulder. "I even thought of a slogan for my campaign buttons. Listen to this

ROSIE SWANSON—FOR YOUR TUMMY'S SAKE."

Maxie tapped his chin and thought it over. "Hmmm. Not bad. Maybe we could make them in the shape of little stomachs. Like those pink tummies they show on Pepto-Bismol commercials. What do you think?"

What did I think? I loved it so much I lifted him right off the floor and give him a giant hug.

Maxie kept his arms stiffly at his sides like a statue. He really hates being picked up. Last year a couple of sixth-graders held him over their heads and passed him around the playground, and it's left him a little bitter.

After I put him down, the three of us sat on my floor and tried to come up with slogans and poster ideas. I made Earl my official art director. Art is Earl's best subject. You should see the stuff he draws. One time he drew a picture of a B-52 bomber blowing up the school that practically looked real.

Anyway, he started doodling a little bit, and in no time at all, he came up with the first poster idea of the day. It was really a neat one, too. It was a picture of this fighter plane dropping a bomb on a drippy carton of milk. Across the top of the poster he printed:

ROSIE SAYS:
NUKE WARM MILK.

I leaned over to hug him, but he pointed his finger at me and said, "Don't even think about it, missy."

45

After that, things got really hard. For the rest of the afternoon, the three of us drove ourselves nuts trying to come up with clever slogans and poems about cafeteria food. We wanted to mention all of the food that kids hate most, but none of it seemed to rhyme.

Earl kept saying, "I'd rather eat a parrot than a carrot." I had to hit him to get him to stop.

Anyway, after about two hours, we were all starting to get headaches, when suddenly Maxie sat up and blurted out,

> "The french fries are fine,
> The fruit cup is better,
> But don't eat the peas,
> Or you'll ralph on your sweater."

I grinned. "That's good, Maxie. I mean it. That's really—"

Before I could finish, another poem popped right out of his mouth:

> "Please don't make us
> Eat Salisbury steakus!"

He motioned toward my notebook. "Quick! Write these down! I think I'm having a burst of genius here or something."

I grabbed my pad and wrote. Then I held on to my pencil and waited. But Maxie's spurt seemed to be over.

"Come on. Keep going," I urged. "What about that gooshy meat?"

"Yeah," said Earl. "The Alpo Platter. The menu called it meatloaf but it smelled more like feetloaf."

We all cracked up. I picked up my pencil and wrote:

The meatloaf
Smells like feetloaf!

Earl took out a piece of paper and drew a smelly foot on a dinner plate. Then he covered it with gravy and drew a lump of mashed potatoes on the side.

The whole time he was drawing, I was laughing. "That looks almost as gross as those corn dogs they had on Friday. Ever wonder about those things? I mean, what the heck are they, anyway? They look like—"

Earl covered his mouth and shook his head. "Please," he begged. "Don't."

After that, the three of us started wondering about corn dogs and what they were made of and stuff. Then Maxie and I began making

up this funny gross poem about them. It made
Earl queasy, but he still laughed. It ended up
being our best idea of the day. A giant poem
called "Dear Mr. Corn Dog":

> Dear Mr. Corn Dog,
> What are you . . . *really*?
> Your inside is meaty,
> Your outside is mealy.
>
> Are you a yo-yo?
> Was it a clue?
> You went down at lunch,
> And you came up at two?
>
> Now you look worse
> Than you did when I ate you.
> I've splattered your batter,
> And now, dog, I hate you.
>
> I'm here in the bathroom,
> I'm still feeling sick.
> And all I've got left
> Of my lunch is your stick.
>
> Dear Mr. Corn Dog,
> I'm not being nosy,
> But what are you . . . *really*?
> Sincerely yours,
>   Rosie

Star-Spangled Me

☆

It was the day before the "Meet the Candidates" meeting, and I have to admit, I was really getting excited about things. Earl and Maxie and I had spent hours making posters. And I just couldn't stop thinking about what a hit they would be when I finally got to hang them in the halls. I mean, I knew that my poems were disgusting and all. But no one likes "disgusting" more than fourth-graders.

I guess you could say that everything was going so well I was feeling sort of spunky. And sometimes when you're feeling spunky, it's easy to start bragging a teeny bit. 'Specially when you're standing directly behind Alan Allen in the drinking fountain line. And he looks right at you. And he doesn't even say hello. Something like that can even make you mad, if you want to know the truth.

Smug. That's how he was acting. *Smug* is a word I learned from Maxie. It means that you're so self-confident you're sickening. Also, you go around with this certain *look* on your face. Like you're almost grinning, but not quite. It's the kind of look that makes people want to smack you.

I didn't smack him, though. Instead, I tapped him on the shoulder. "Soooo, how's the old campaign going, Al?" I asked spunkily. "Been working on your posters much?"

Alan stared at me a second. Like he was trying to figure out who I was. Then he shrugged. "I don't know. Not really."

"Oh?" I replied, raising my eyebrows. "Well, you better get busy. 'Cause guess what? I've been working on *my* posters a lot."

Alan didn't reply.

"A *real* lot," I added. "See, I've got these two fifth-graders helping me. Maybe you've heard of them. Earl Wilber and Maxie Zuckerman? Earl's like the best artist in the entire fifth grade. And Maxie's like an Einstein or something. So you can imagine the great poster ideas we've come up with."

Alan bent over and drank from the fountain. I knew he was listening, though. I could **50** *tell* he was listening.

I bent over with him. "Unfortunately, I can't tell you what the posters are about, Al. I'm keeping all my campaign ideas a secret until the 'Meet the Candidates' meeting tomorrow."

Alan stopped drinking for a second. Then he started again.

"I can tell you this much, though. It's a great campaign. And that's not bragging, either. My grandfather says something's only bragging if it's not true. And what I'm saying is all true, Al. I've got a great campaign. Seriously. I do."

Finally, Alan stood back up and wiped the water off his mouth. "Gee," he said. "I'm really scared."

Then he turned and ran back out to the soccer field.

I couldn't help smiling a little bit. 'Cause most of the time when kids say they're not scared, it's only because they are.

I leaned down and got a drink of water.

As I was swallowing I felt a tap on my arm. "Hey. What's going on? What were you guys talking about?"

I turned around. Summer Lynne Jones was standing right behind me. She must have been trying to snoop.

I looked at her a second. Then I *almost* grinned, but not quite.

"Ohhhh . . . nothing," I answered at last. "I think Alan's just a little worried about my campaign, that's all. I was just telling him how great it was going and all."

I paused. "I mean *really* great, too."

Then I smiled and started to stroll away. "Well . . . ta ta," I sang.

I fluttered my fingers and waved when I said "ta ta."

It was wonderful.

That afternoon Granddad picked me up from school. My mother said I could buy a special new outfit to wear to the candidates' meeting, so Granddad offered to take me to the mall.

When it comes to shopping, my grandfather and I get along a lot better than my mom and I do. That's because my mother is impossible to shop with. She's always trying to buy me things a kindergarten kid would wear. Also, if I find two outfits that I really love, she almost never lets me get both of them. Not even if I cry and promise not to ask for another thing for the rest of my life.

My grandfather is a lot nicer. He just finds

a chair, sits down, and holds my jacket while I try on whatever I want. Sometimes he goes to sleep. Once, a security guard thought he was dead and poked him with a plastic hanger.

Not this time, though. This time I was so speedy my grandfather didn't even have a chance to get comfortable. The outfit I wanted was right on the mannequin in the girls' department. It was a red, white, and blue sweater and a matching navy-blue skirt. The perfect colors for an election.

It looked great on me too. When I came out of the dressing room, the saleslady whistled and said I looked like "a million bucks."

"I'm running for president of my fourth-grade class," I informed her.

She grinned. "Well, in that outfit you can't lose, honey. Right, Gramps?"

Granddad looked up and frowned.

I leaned across the counter. "He hates being called Gramps," I whispered.

The lady just shrugged and said, "Cash or charge?"

Anyway, as it turned out, my mother loved the outfit as much as I did. The next morning she even fixed my hair in a French braid and tied it with red, white, and blue satin ribbons.

When I got to Maxie's house, Earl said I looked like the Star-Spangled Banner. He took off his baseball cap when he said it, so I knew it was a compliment.

Before we left, he dug into his jeans and held his hand out to me. "Here," he said. "I found these this morning. They were growing through a crack in my driveway."

He opened his fist. Lying in his palm were two limp four-leaf clovers.

"You know . . . for good luck," he said quietly.

I started to take both of them, but Earl shook his head. "Only one," he told me. Then he put the other one back in his pocket.

It made me smile.

Finally, we started to walk. "Well, I guess this is it, huh, guys? Today's the big day, right? I hope I do okay at the meeting and everything. I mean, I hope I don't say anything too stupid."

I paused and waited for them to say, "Don't worry, Rosie. You won't." But as usual, they didn't take the hint.

Maxie clutched the posters he was carrying tighter to his body. Even though they were wrapped in black plastic, he kept them well hidden. He was really acting strange. Except for "Hello," he'd hardly said a word.

"I'm sure they're going to like our poems," I babbled excitedly. "I mean, I think this food idea is going to knock their socks off, don't you? That's what my mother calls it when you really surprise people. She calls it knocking their socks off.

"And I don't want you guys to worry, either," I went on. "Just because you're in fifth grade and I'm only in fourth doesn't mean you can't help me be president. You can be my advisers."

Maxie forced a smile. Meanwhile, Earl was holding the bag of campaign buttons so tightly his fingers were turning white. It was pretty clear that neither one of them was used to keeping secrets. Not like *I* was, anyway.

When we got to school, the bell was already ringing. Maxie and Earl seemed relieved to hand me the posters and campaign buttons.

Earl wiped the sweat from the top of his lip. He rocked back and forth for a few seconds like there was something important on his mind. Then he just turned and hurried through the door.

Maxie was already long gone.

The candidates' meeting was at nine-thirty. Mr. Jolly dismissed me at nine o'clock so I could "get ready." In a way, it was sort of insulting. Couldn't he see that I was already *ready*? I was dressed like the Star-Spangled Banner. How much better can you look than that?

I didn't make a big deal about it, though. I just went into the girls' bathroom and sat on the sink for a while. Then finally, I wandered over to the media center.

Nic and Vic Timmerman were already there. Their hair was wet and freshly parted like they had just gotten out of the shower. They were searching for their places at the long "candidates' table" in the front of the room.

I thought about talking to them. But then Louise the Disease came in, so I talked to her instead. I know this sounds mean, but I'd rather catch a cold than be seen with two boys with slick hair and matching bow ties.

One by one, the other candidates came in and found their names at the big table. All the candidates for class secretary were at one end, and all the presidents were at the other end. Treasurers and vice presidents were in the middle.

Summer Lynne Jones sat in the chair on my right at the very end of the table. Even though it was sort of chilly outside, she was wearing a bright-yellow sundress and sandals with lacy yellow socks. I think she wanted to look "summery."

"You look like a flag," she said when she sat down.

"Thank you," I replied stiffly. But this time I was pretty sure it wasn't a compliment. Competitors almost never compliment each other. Like you never really hear boxers get into the ring and say, "Hey, Rocky, love your shorts."

Alan Allen was the last candidate to arrive. He strolled in the room real casual-like and sat down on my left. He waved to his friends on the floor, and they laughed a little. Then he looked over at me and gave me this super-weird grin.

All of a sudden, Mrs. Munson clapped her hands together to begin the meeting.

"May I have your attention please?" she asked. "As your teachers have explained, this morning we are going to have an opportunity to meet the candidates running for class office. During the past few days, we have been talking to you about the political process and how it works. As we have told you, the job you have as voters is the most important job there is. You have the awesome responsibility of choosing the best person for each office. And so it's up to you to find out as much about the candidates and their views as you can.

"This morning the candidates are going to introduce themselves to you and tell you a little bit about themselves and their campaigns. We will begin with Roxanne Handleman, who is running for class secretary."

Roxanne gasped. "No way!" she sputtered.

Mrs. Munson frowned. "Excuse me, Roxanne?" she said.

"Why me? Why do I have to go first? How come we can't just raise our hands when we're ready to talk? I thought we were gonna get to raise our hands."

Mr. Jolly walked over to Roxanne and leaned down. "There's nothing to be nervous about," he said quietly. "We just want to know a little bit about you and why you're running. We talked about this before, remember?"

"Yeah, I know. But nobody said I had to go first. I thought we were gonna get to raise our hands when we were ready."

Mr. Jolly narrowed his eyes and raised his eyebrows at the same time. I don't know how he does this, but it looks very scary. *"Roxanne,"* he said sternly.

Finally, Roxanne stood up. "Okay, I'll do it. But I still don't think this is fair."

She took a deep breath. "My name is Roxanne Handleman and I'm running for class secretary because, well, I just wanted to, that's all. I mean, why do I need a good reason? It's a free country, isn't it? Lots of people do stuff without good reasons. Like my brother is late for dinner almost every single night. And he almost never has a good reason. But he still gets to eat. 'Cause like I said, it's a free country. And anyway, just because I don't have a good reason doesn't mean I wouldn't be a good secretary. 'Cause I would. It's just that I thought we were gonna get to raise our hands, that's all."

Roxanne sat down and put her head on the table. It made a loud clunk when it hit. She covered up with her arms.

Next to her, Karla something jumped right up. She didn't even wait to be called on.

"My name is Karla Ungerman and I'm running for class secretary because my mother— Mrs. Sharla Ungerman—is a secretary at the high school, and she's teaching me how to type, and I'm very organized, and ever since first grade I've always gotten straight A's in English and penmanship."

Karla sat down for a second, then popped

right back up again. "Oops! Almost forgot—I also get A's in spelling."

This time when she sat, she smoothed her dress neatly and lowered herself gracefully into her chair.

Roxanne raised her head and glared at Karla meanly. "Well, big woo," she said right out loud.

The candidates for treasurer came next. Louise the Disease stood up and showed everyone her new calculator. "I just got this for my birthday," she announced proudly.

Then she sort of dangled it in front of Robert Moneypenny's face. "And I know how to use it too, guy."

Robert just grinned. He leaned his chair back on two legs and raised his fists in the air.

"Robert Moneypenny for treasurer!" he declared.

Then all the boys started waving their fists too. And they began making this gorilla noise that sounded like "who who who who who who."

During the noise, Vic Timmerman stood up and blurted, "I'm Victor Timmerman and I'm a whiz with numbers." I'm pretty sure no one heard him, though.

I don't remember what the candidates for vice president said. By that time I was too nervous to pay much attention. All I know for sure is that when we got to the presidents, Summer Lynne Jones said a few words and then tossed her long blond hair around for a while.

After that, Alan stood up and the room practically went wild. I mean it. Kids started chanting his name and they wouldn't stop.

"Allllan   Allllan   Allllan   Allllan   Allllan . . ."

Finally, Alan raised his hands to quiet the crowd. Then he looked down at me and gave me that same superweird grin again. A second later, he pulled a piece of paper from his shirt pocket and began to read:

"The french fries are fine,
The fruit cup is better,
But don't eat the peas,
Or you'll ralph on your sweater."

He looked up from his paper and beamed. "Alan Allen for better lunches!" he shouted.

I almost fell off my chair.

Hard Feelings

☆

I sat there for a few seconds, in shock I guess you'd say. Then suddenly, I sprang right out of my seat. "Wait a minute! Hold it! Stop! That was *my* poem!"

Then I started yelling, "He stole it! He stole it! He stole it!"

Unfortunately, "He stole it!" turned out to be my whole speech.

Mrs. Munson rushed up to the candidates' table and ordered me to take my seat "this instant, young lady.

"We will get to the bottom of this later," she said, through clenched teeth.

I guess I must have sat down. But I really don't remember much. I was boiling over. I mean it. I was madder than I've ever been in my whole life.

The meeting came to a quick close. Then Mrs. Munson and Mr. Jolly met with Alan and me.

"Alan?" Mr. Jolly said. "You want to tell us about the poem?" Then he folded his arms and waited until Alan admitted that it had been mine.

"See?" I shouted. "I *told* you he stole it!"

"I did not!" Alan protested. "I didn't steal anything! One of her friends told it to me. If you don't believe me, just ask him. It was that geeky fifth-grader. And anyway, I thought it would be okay. My father said that in political campaigns, people use each other's ideas all the time."

Mr. Jolly glared at Alan meanly. You could tell he was really mad. "Stealing a poem wasn't what your father meant, Alan. I think you know that. That poem was Rosie's. You owe her a big apology."

I stamped my foot. "No, Mr. Jolly! No! That's not what I want. I don't *want* a stupid apology. Saying he's sorry won't change anything. Just don't let him campaign for better cafeteria food, that's all. That was *my* idea. Just tell him he can't use it."

Mr. Jolly was still glaring at Alan angrily. Mrs. Munson was, too. She had her arms crossed and was tapping her foot on the floor. They weren't *saying* anything, though. Why didn't they just tell him he couldn't use my ideas?

Finally, Mr. Jolly stood up and ran his fingers through his hair. "I don't know, Rosie. I just don't know," he said, sounding frustrated. "We all agree that it was wrong that Alan recited your poem. But I'm not sure that I can absolutely forbid him to campaign for better cafeteria food."

A knot formed in my stomach. "Yes you *can*. You're a *teacher*. You can absolutely forbid anything you want to."

Mrs. Munson stopped tapping her foot and sat on the edge of the table. "I'm afraid Alan's father may be right about this," she said. "This is politics. And in politics, if one candidate comes up with a really good idea, you can't keep the other candidates from using it too."

She leaned down and tried to look me in the eye. I think she was trying to be warm or something.

"You see what I'm saying, don't you, Rose? Let's say that two men are running for President of the United States, and one of them decides he'll lower taxes. Well, if the other candidate thinks that lowering taxes will be a popular idea with the voters, then he might begin to campaign for it too. And he's *allowed* to do that."

64   I turned my eyes away from her.

Mr. Jolly sighed deeply. "Look, Rosie. I know exactly how you feel about what happened today. And we certainly won't let Alan use your poems or copy your poster ideas. But if he comes up with some food ideas of his own, we can't stop him from using them. Mrs. Munson is right. If Alan thinks it's going to be popular, then he's allowed to jump on the bandwagon."

I didn't know what a bandwagon was. And I didn't care.

Alan was practically puffing out with glee. You should have seen him. You could have popped him with a pin.

He stood up and held out his hand to me. "Sorry about the poem thing. No hard feelings, okay?" he said.

I stared at his hand. "Yes there are, Alan. There're lots of hard feelings."

Then I turned to Mr. Jolly. "And guess what? No one knows *exactly how I feel*, either."

After that, I just walked away.

I found them on the playground at recess. They were crouching behind a tree near the swings.

As soon as I spotted them I took off as fast

as I could go. I was shouting and waving my fists in the air. I'm not that strong, but my fists are bony, so they hurt when they connect.

"You can't hide from me! I see you! I see you!"

Maxie watched me coming. At first it looked like he might make a run for it. But then he just folded his arms and leaned back against the tree. "What are you yelling about? We weren't hiding. Why would we be hiding?"

I looked down at Earl. He was doubled over into a little ball and had totally covered up with his sweater.

I yanked the sweater off his head. "It was supposed to be a secret, Earl! It was supposed to be a secret!"

Furiously, I took his four-leaf clover out of my pocket and threw it at his face.

It hit him on the cheek. Earl stared at it on the ground. He looked sick and sad and ashamed all at the same time. "I knew those stupid clovers wouldn't work," he muttered.

He looked up. "I'm sorry," he said weakly. "They made me tell."

I bit my lip to keep from crying. I'm not a
crybaby or anything. It's just that I was so

disappointed in him, that's all. Right up until he said it, I kept hoping that it wouldn't be true.

"Who?" I wanted to know. "Who made you tell them?"

His answer took me by surprise.

"Summer Lynne Jones," he said. "Summer Lynne Jones and that friend of hers. The pretty one with the long black hair. It was them. They ran up behind me while I was walking home from school yesterday and started asking a bunch of stuff about your campaign."

I rolled my eyes. "Like what *kind* of stuff?"

He shrugged. "You know. Like what kind of posters I was drawing . . . stuff like that. She said that Alan Allen told her I was helping you with your posters, and she was wondering what kind of junk I was drawing for you."

"And so you *told* her? You just spilled your guts about our campaign? Just like that?"

"No!" he exclaimed. "I didn't tell her anything! I said we were keeping it a secret until the candidates' meeting."

I folded my arms. "So then what?"

Earl swallowed hard. "Well, we were just standing around in the grass and then the one with the long black hair—the pretty one—

patted the ground. You know . . . for me to sit down."

"So?"

"So I sat."

"And?"

Earl lowered his voice again. "And then Summer asked me if I was ticklish. And even though I said no, she started tickling me anyway. And then the one with the long black hair joined in. And the two of them just kept tickling and tickling. And they said they wouldn't stop until I told them about your posters."

I couldn't stand to listen to this. I covered my face with my hands. "Oh Earl."

"I couldn't help it, Rosie. I started getting wheezy. You know how plugged up I get. And I didn't have my squeezy nose drops or my mouth inhaler with me, either. So I couldn't breathe at all. I *had* to tell them. It was life or death."

I was angry all over again.

"No it wasn't, Earl! Your nose is no excuse. What kind of traitor spills his guts to the enemy and then runs back to camp and says, 'Sorry, General, I was plugged up'?

"Do you know what happened because of you, Earl? Your giggly little girlfriends told Alan Allen all about my campaign. And Alan

Allen stood right up in front of the entire fourth grade this morning and recited one of my poems. And he said he was going to work for better lunches."

Tears started to fill my eyes. "Darn it, Earl! Why did you have to tell?"

Earl sat there for a second, just sort of staring off into space. Then he got a funny look on his face. "No. Wait a minute. That can't be right. How could he have recited one of our poems? I didn't tell Summer Lynne *any* of our poems."

"Yes you did! You did too, Earl! You told her the one about the fruit cup and the french fries, because that's the poem he recited. And if you didn't tell her, then how else would Alan Allen have known it?"

Just then, Maxie started walking toward the school. He didn't say a word. He just started to walk.

I grabbed his arm. He spun around and looked at me.

That's when I knew.

"You," I said in amazement. *"You're* the one who did it."

Maxie was practically glaring at me. Glaring . . . you know, like *he* was more angry than *I* was.

"Yeah . . . okay. It was me. So what? I don't

care what you say, either, Rosie. I'm sick of getting insulted by kids like Alan Allen. Sixth-graders are bad enough. But he's only a *fourth-grader!*"

Maxie's eyes narrowed. "He called me Poindexter! And a dweeb. And he said if I was such a brainiac, then how come I couldn't figure out how to grow? *Even a stupid gorilla knows how to grow,* he says to me."

Maxie pointed to Earl. "And he made fun of Earl, too. He said Earl couldn't draw worth spit. *Earl Wilber is a doofus,* he says. *My posters are going to kill your posters. Kill 'em, Zuckerman,* he says.

"So I just try to be cool about it, you know? And I say, 'Yeah? We'll just see about that, Alan.' And I start to walk away.

"Except then, a couple of his friends grab me and twirl me around in a circle until I can't walk straight. And then Alan puts his arm around my shoulders like we were pals. *Okay,* he says. *I'll make you a deal. I'll tell you a secret about me, and then you can tell me your campaign secret. That way we'll be even.*

"Then he whispers this stupid secret about how he took a soccer ball from Mort's Sports Store when he was in first grade.

"So I say, 'Big deal, Alan. What good's a

stupid secret like that going to do us? I'm not telling you anything.'

"And that's when Alan really gets mad. And he grabs the front of my shirt with both of his fists and starts slinging me around a little bit. And he's getting me totally wrinkled. And so I say, 'Knock it off, Alan. My mother just ironed this shirt!'

"And he looks at me like I was a lunatic or something. And he says, *God! How can such a skinny wimp be such a giant dork? Huh? I mean, how is that even scientifically possible?*

"And then he hits himself in the head and says, *What the heck was I so worried about? There's no way in the world that you and that fat tub of goo, Earl Wilber, will be able to get your geeky girlfriend elected president of the fourth grade. No way.*

"After that, he let go of me and shoved me backward. And I was so mad I could spit. And so I took a giant step right into his face. And then I stood on my toes until our noses were almost touching, and I said, 'Oh yeah? Well, laugh about this, you snool. 'Cause this is what's going to blow your campaign right out of the water!' And then I blurted out the fruit cup poem."

71

Maxie stopped and took a breath. "And I'm

sorry, okay? I'm really sorry, but it just came out. And I'm just sick of being picked on, that's all. I'm just sick of it."

The bell rang. Maxie and Earl didn't move. Neither did I.

I felt all droopy and limp inside. I sat down in the grass and pulled my knees up to hide my face.

Earl came over and gently tapped me on the shoulder. "Come on. We'd better go."

I brushed his hand away.

"So go," I said.

And they did.

The American Way

☆

I didn't speak to Maxie or Earl for two days.
I wanted to hold out longer, but I couldn't.
Knowing that they were walking to school
without me was driving me crazy. I was almost positive that they weren't using the
crosswalks.

Friday morning, I finally showed up at
Maxie's house. It was kind of awkward at first.
We mostly just stood around and looked at
each other. We haven't really been friends that
long, so we're still learning how to do it.

I smiled a little. "Hi," I said at last.

Maxie waved stiffly. "Hi."

A second later, Earl did all three. He smiled
and waved and said, "Hi." Then he bent over
and butted me with his head. I don't know
why. It's just the way his mind works. It did
the trick, though. We loosened up after that.   **73**

We didn't have a big discussion about what happened or anything. I mostly just told them to forget about it. It was big of me, I thought. I told them that, too. "This is big of me," I said.

I didn't tell them that I thought I might be partly to blame. I have a feeling I was, though. 'Cause maybe if I hadn't been feeling so "spunky" at the water fountain that day, none of this would have happened in the first place. Maybe.

Anyway, I was very glad to have my friends back again. At school, things were getting harder and harder to deal with. Alan's posters were going up all over the place. Most of them were about food, too. Just like I knew they would be.

They weren't as good as mine, of course. Even Norman Beeman said so. He plodded right up to me in the hall and said, "Don't worry. Your posters are way neater than his."

"Thank you, Norman," I said. "Love your boots."

You could tell that Alan hadn't really worked very hard on his campaign. Most of his posters were just boring old pictures of pizza cut out of magazines. His slogan was stupid, too:

PIZZA AND COKE?
GIVE ALAN YOUR VOTE!

Coke and *vote* don't even rhyme. And here's another dumb thing. Alan's campaign buttons were napkins.

Even Summer Lynne Jones' campaign buttons were better than napkins. Unlike Alan, she had decided not to steal my campaign ideas. She didn't do it to be nice, though. She said she thought my food poems were revolting.

Most of her posters were pictures of people at the beach. You know . . . people doing "summery" things. At the top of every poster there was a picture of the sun wearing sunglasses. It said:

KIDS LOVE SUMMER!

Like a lot of girls, she dotted her *i*'s with little hearts. Talk about revolting.

Her campaign buttons were little paper-doll swimsuits made of different-colored construction paper. They even had tabs on them like real paper-doll clothes.

The girls loved them. When Summer passed them out after the candidates' meeting, I could actually hear girls squealing because they were so cute. Squealing like little pigs.

Still, out of all the candidates running for office, Louise the Disease's campaign was the stupidest. All her posters said the very same thing.

LOUISE MARIE SMYTHE—
SHE COMES WITH HER OWN CALCULATOR.

It made her sound like a Christmas doll or something.

She didn't stand a chance against Robert Moneypenny. His posters were cooler than anything. Each one had a snapshot of Robert leaning back in an easy chair, with his feet propped up on a big desk. And underneath each picture it said:

MONEYPENNY FOR TREASURER
THE NAME SAYS IT ALL . . .

Except for Alan Allen, Karla something turned out to be the meanest person running for office. Her posters were sort of vicious, if you want to know the truth. They said stuff like:

ROXANNE HANDLEMAN GOT A "D"
IN PENMANSHIP.

And:

ASK ROXANNE ABOUT HER GRADE IN SPELLING.

They didn't stay up long, though. As soon as Mr. Jolly saw them, he called a short candidates' meeting and told us that dirty campaigning and "mudslinging" were not allowed. He said that even though it happens in *real* campaigns, elementary schools should have higher standards than our nation's leaders.

Anyway, I never thought I'd say this, but making posters turned out to be one of the easiest parts of running for office. The hardest part was how I had to go around being *nice* to people all the time. And how I had to always keep *smiling*. I'm not kidding. I even had to smile at kids who make me puke.

Maxie said it's called "sucking up." He said it's the American way.

Sometimes I smiled till my cheeks ached. Twice I had to go into the girls' room and take baby aspirin. But even then, it didn't seem like it was making much of a difference.

"I don't think this *cheery* stuff is working," I reported glumly to Maxie one afternoon. "Hardly anybody ever smiles back. When you're too happy, kids think you're a sicko or something. Yesterday I was standing around grinning at a bunch of kids in the lunch line, 77 and this boy I didn't even know told me I was giving him the creeps."

Maxie wasn't very sympathetic. "I don't care. It doesn't matter. You *have* to keep smiling. Smiling is one of the three main rules of politics: (1) smile, (2) have a firm hand-shake, and (3) never wear a bad toupee."

Judith Topper was the hardest person for me to smile at. Just in case you forgot, Judith is the jerky, creepy, goony girl who sits right in front of me.

Every day she came to school wearing one of Alan's stupid campaign napkins. I'm posi-tive she only did it to annoy me. Sometimes she'd even point at it and say, "Alan says we're gonna have pizza every single Friday. That's why I'm voting for *him* and not *you.*"

I tried not to let her see how much it both-ered me. Mostly I just shrugged and said, "I know, Judith. But Alan would never even have *thought* of the pizza idea if it wasn't for me."

"Would've too," she would say.

Then after she turned back around, I would make a gross face. The one where I pull down the bottoms of my eyes and stretch my mouth out with my thumbs.

I never let her see me, though. 'Cause here's the worst part of all. Even though I can't stand

Judith Topper's guts, I still wanted her to vote for me.

I'm not proud about it, but it's true. That's what happens in politics. Even if a disgusting green slimeball oozed under the classroom door, you'd still want it to vote for you.

Stuff like that can make you very mixed up inside. And guess what else? Sometimes when you're very mixed up inside, you do things you know you shouldn't do.

I've never told anybody this. Not even Maxie. But I wanted Judith Topper's vote so bad I let her look at the answers on my state capitals test. I did. I actually let that creep *cheat* off me.

I still think about it a lot. About how I pretended to drop my pencil on the floor that day. And how I leaned down to pick it up as slowly as I could. To give her time, you know? Time to see almost any answer she wanted.

I'd even written VOTE FOR ROSIE in the margin of my paper, so she would understand that we were sort of helping each other out here.

I'm still not exactly sure what happened. Maybe it's just hard to read state capitals when they're upside down or something. But Judith didn't pass the test. She put down that **79** the capital of Delaware was Rover, instead of Dover. Like Delaware would actually name its capital after a dog. Also, she wrote that the capital of Idaho was Potato.

But what made me the sickest was that the very next morning she *still* came to school wearing one of those stupid napkins on her collar.

I put one of my little pink stomach buttons on her desk so she could switch. But instead of pinning it on, she picked it up by the very edge—like it was dirty or something—and then she dropped it on the floor.

"No offense," she said, wrinkling up her nose. "But these little stomachs are the most disgusting campaign buttons I've ever seen."

This time I didn't even *think* about being nice. "Yeah, well, they're better than that bib *you've* got on, Judith. That's what that stupid napkin looks like, you know. It looks just like a baby bib."

Judith smiled meanly. Then she started singing, "You're gonna lose." Only she sang it real loud and slow, like, "YOU'RE GONNA LUUUU-OOOOZE. YOU'RE GONNA LUUUU-OOOOZE."

Two rows over, Billie Ray Carver grabbed a pencil and hopped up on his chair. He pretended to be her conductor. You know, the orchestra guy with the stick.

I hate Billie Ray Carver. Not quite as much as Judith Topper, but still a very, very lot.

Sometimes when he walks past my desk, I hold my breath. He doesn't smell bad or anything. I just don't like to breathe in the air he's stirred up. It's filled with BRc's—Billie Ray's cooties. And I don't want them getting into my nostrils.

Anyway, the stupid thing was that the whole time Billie Ray Carver was pretending to be a conductor, he was wearing one of *my* campaign buttons. Not on his collar, though. He was wearing it on his stomach.

Billie Ray really loved my buttons. Maxie said he was the best advertisement we had. "Face it, Rosie," he told me. "The jerk's got a lot of friends. You've *got* to be nice to Billie Ray Carver. I mean it, too. Even if it *kills* you."

And so that afternoon, when we went out to the playground for recess and I saw Billie Ray Carver spit on the swing set, I didn't say a word. Not one word.

He knew I was watching him, too. "Hey, Swanson," he hollered. "Want to see something funny?"

Then he called to this new girl in our class named Anna Havana. "Hey, Anna. Come over here! I'll push you!"

And so Anna Havana went over and sat down right on the swing with the spit. And I didn't even try to warn her. I just kept my mouth shut. And I watched.

And I told myself it was no big deal, you know? 'Cause Billie Ray was important to my campaign. And anyway, Anna's dress would dry in no time at all, right? I mean, it was only a little blob of spit and all. Right?

I'm not saying I felt good about any of this. I'm just telling you what happened, that's all.

After recess, Billie Ray Carver stopped by my desk. "Did you see that, Swanson?" he asked. "Man . . . girls are such *suckers*."

I tried not to breathe in his air. "Yeah, well, if girls are such suckers, then how come you're voting for one, Billie Ray?" I asked.

For a second, he looked really confused. Then he glanced down at my campaign button and started to laugh.

"What? Are you crazy? Just because you have the grossest campaign buttons doesn't mean I'd ever *vote* for you.

"News flash, Swanson. You're a dorky girl.

No boy in his right mind would vote for a

four-eyed, geeky girl. Not in a zillion jillion years. And anyway, in case you haven't heard, Alan Allen is going to get us pizza and Coke on Fridays."

Then Billie Ray Carver leaned so close to me that billions of his cooties poured into my nostrils. "Allllan . . . Allllan . . . Allllan . . . Allllan . . . Allllan," he began to chant.

Judith Topper spun around in her chair and joined in.

"Allllan . . . Allllan . . . Allllan . . . Allllan," they sang together. And they just kept it up and kept it up until I didn't think I could stand it anymore.

Where was Mr. Jolly? Why wasn't he in the room yet?

"Allllan . . . Allllan . . . Allllan . . ."

They wanted me to cry. I know they did. I didn't do it, though. The inside of my throat ached from trying to hold back the tears, but I still didn't cry.

And then all of a sudden, this really weird thing happened. One of my hands snuck into my desk and started crawling all around in there. Searching for something. You know, like it had two little eyes and a brain of its own.

And then—way in the back, under my

geography workbook—my hand finally found what it was looking for. It found my yellow "secret informer" notepad.

And suddenly, I felt myself start to relax.

And then my throat wasn't sore anymore.

I smiled.

I had a plan.

Moon Men

☆

The plan was simple. So simple I wondered why I hadn't thought of it before.

The voters had a job to do, but they just weren't doing it. Hadn't they heard what Mrs. Munson had said at the meeting? They were supposed to be finding out as much as they could about the candidates so they could choose the *best* person for the office.

But instead, kids like Billie Ray Carver and Judith Topper were going to vote for Alan Allen just because he was a boy . . . or even worse, because of a pizza idea that he practically stole from me. And it just wasn't fair!

I was the best choice for president. Me! Rosebud Swanson! I was honest and law-abiding and very, very smiley.

Alan Allen was none of those things. And if the voters weren't going to find out the truth 85 about him for themselves, then I would simply have to help them out a little bit.

As soon as the coast was clear, I pulled out my notepad and wrote four short notes. They were all the same:

Dear Fourth-Grade Friend,
Alan Allen stole a soccer ball from Mort's Sports. Is this the kind of person you want to elect for President of the Fourth Grade?

> Sincerely yours,
> The Committee Who Wants
> You to Be a Good Voter
> and Not Just Vote for the
> Kid Who is the Most Popular

There, I said to myself. I folded each one separately and stuffed it deep into my skirt pocket. There.

Knowing what I was going to do made me scared and excited at the same time. All I had to do was "deliver" one note to each fourth-grade classroom. After that, the news would spread like crazy. And as long as I was careful, no one would ever know that it was me who started it all.

Disguise the notes, Rosie. I don't know
where the idea came from. It just popped into

my head like one of those little light bulbs in the comic strips.

Disguise the notes so no one can tell they're from you.

I pulled them out of my pocket again and hid them on my lap. Then carefully, I opened each one up and did this really clever thing. I dotted all the *i*'s with little hearts. You know, just like Summer Lynne Jones and all her ditsy friends.

Coming up with clever stuff like that is what makes me a good secret agent. Seriously. It's like a gift or something.

I was just stuffing the last note back into my pocket, when the dismissal bell rang. I didn't leave, though. I stayed in my seat and waited for everyone to clear out of the room.

It seemed to take forever. This kid named William Washington would *not* go home. He kept following Mr. Jolly around and around the room, telling him some stupid story about how his grandmother has a potato chip that looks like Elvis Presley.

It took ten minutes before William wrapped up his potato chip story. Meanwhile, I pretended to be cleaning out my desk. Finally, Mr. Jolly walked William into the hall. That's when I made my move.

In a flash, I pulled one of the notes out of my pocket and put it on Neil McNutt's chair. Neil McNutt is the biggest gossip in the entire fourth grade. I'm not kidding. Neil spreads news like wildfire.

After that, I grabbed my jacket and hurried out the door. Then as I walked down the hall I ducked into each of the other fourth-grade classrooms and deposited a note on the closest chair.

This might sound risky, but it wasn't. Two of the teachers were out of their rooms. The other one was standing at the sink. It looked like she was trying to get glue out of her hair or something. She never even turned around.

Once I got outside the building, I started to run. I didn't stop, either. Not until I was all the way home. Then I hit the front door, ran straight up to my room, and locked myself inside.

I huffed and puffed and tried to catch my breath. "The voters will thank you for this," I whispered to myself.

Downstairs, I could hear my mother rattling around in the kitchen. I unlocked my door and went down. If I don't say hello to my mother when I come home from school, she comes stalking me.

I strolled into the kitchen and grabbed an apple out of the fruit bowl on the table. "Hi," I said casually.

Mom was making a salad for dinner. She smiled back. Then the two of us had our usual after-school conversation.

"Where've you been?"

"Nowhere."

"What'cha been up to?"

"Nothin'."

"How was school today?"

" 'kay."

"How's the campaign going?"

My stomach tightened a little.

" 'kay."

Mom nodded. "Good." Then she went back to her salad.

For a while, I just sat there drumming my fingers on the tabletop. And whenever she looked at me, I smiled. You know, so she wouldn't think there was anything wrong.

There was, though. For some reason, my stomach wouldn't loosen up and my hands started to feel real clammy. I guess my nerves were finally starting to catch up with me or something. That happens sometimes. You're real brave at first, and then your nerves catch up with you.

I swallowed. Nothing went down.

"Mom? I've sort of got a question about something, I think," I said at last. "I mean, I'm sure I already know the answer. But I just kind of want your opinion."

" 'bout what?" she replied.

I squirmed a little. How should I put this? How much did I want her to know?

"Uh, well, I don't know. It's sorta about . . ."

I paused to think a second.

". . . moon men, I guess you'd say."

My mother raised her eyebrows. "Moon men?"

"Yeah. It's about moon men. See, I was just wondering what would happen if there was this moon man who wanted to be elected king of the moon. And he was really popular and everything. Only there was something about him that the other moon men didn't know. Something he had done that was sort of . . . bad."

My mother folded her arms. "Like what?"

I squirmed some more. "Oh, I don't know. Something like . . ."

I lowered my voice.

". . . like maybe he had stolen something. I mean, if he had stolen something, and the voters didn't know about it, then somebody ought to tell them. Don't you think?"

My mother walked over and sat down next to me. I had a feeling she knew we weren't talking about moon men.

"What?" she wanted to know.

"What what?" I asked back.

"What did he steal?"

I shrugged my shoulders. "I don't know. Like what if he stole a little moon ball or something? If he stole a little moon ball, then someone should tell the voters. Right? That way they could do their job better. And they wouldn't elect a thief."

My mother leaned back in her chair and looked at the ceiling. She almost always looks at the ceiling when she thinks.

"How long ago did he steal it?" she wanted to know next. "How old was he when it happened?"

I couldn't believe this! Where was she getting all these dumb questions?

"I don't know, Mother," I snapped. "What difference does it make?"

"A lot, Rosie," she replied. "It could make a lot of difference. Maybe he's not really a thief at all. Maybe he just made a mistake and it was a long time ago and he learned his 91 lesson. So maybe now he's just as honest—or even *more* honest—than anyone else on the moon."

I rolled my eyes. "No. That's stupid. How can somebody who's stolen something be more honest than someone who's never stolen anything in her entire life? That's just stupid."

My mom stared at me curiously. Then she took one of those long, deep breaths that mothers always take when they're trying to brace themselves for bad news.

"Okay, kiddo," she said. "Let's have it. What's this all about?"

I stood up. "Nothing. It's not about anything. It was just a stupid question about stupid moon men, and I don't want to talk about it any stupid more."

Then before she could ask any more questions, I ducked out the door and hurried toward the stairs. Halfway there, I looked back over my shoulder. I couldn't believe she wasn't following me. Usually when I act like that, she's all over me like poison ivy.

As soon as I got to my room, I locked my door again. Sometimes adults don't make any sense at all. I mean, who the heck cares how **92** *old* Alan was when he stole the soccer ball?

Even a *baby* thief is still a thief, isn't he? And anyway, it was pretty clear that Alan hadn't learned his lesson about stealing. He'd stolen my poem right out of Maxie's mouth!

Just then there was a knock on my door. I knew it! I knew she'd follow me!

"Rosie? Can I come in? What's wrong? Did one of the other candidates fake something?"

I forced my voice to sound normal. "No. It's nothing. Just never mind, okay? I'm taking a nap."

There was a pause.

"Rosie."

"I'm asleep."

I listened closely. Mom sat down on the floor and leaned her back up against my door.

"Sorry," she said. "But I'm not leaving until you tell me what's going on."

I made a loud snoring sound.

"Come on, Rosie. I want to know. What's going on at school? Maybe I can help."

I covered my head with my blanket. "No you can't," I said finally. "Nobody can. You don't have a magic wand, do you, Mother? Do you have a magic wand that will make me pretty and popular?"

I knew what she would say, of course. It's   **93**

the same thing mothers *always* say at times like this.

"But you *are*, honey," she began. "You're very—"

"No I'm not, Mother!" I interrupted. "I never should have been in this election in the first place. It was a big, giant, stupid mistake. I'm a four-eyed, geeky girl, and no boy in his right mind would ever vote for me. Just ask Billie Ray Carver. *He'll* tell you."

"No, Rosie. That's not true. I'm sure there are plenty of boys who will—"

I put my hands over my ears again. "No there aren't! There are not!"

I started to cry a little bit.

My mother stood up and knocked softly on my door. "Come on. Open up," she said. "I mean it. I want you to let me in."

I sat there for a few seconds. Finally, I wiped my eyes with my blanket and smoothed my hair a little bit.

I opened my door.

Then I let my mother hug me for a very long time.

Like Wildfire

☆

Neil McNutt found my note at 7:55 the next morning. I was still feeling a little mixed up about stuff, but I didn't try to stop what was about to happen. I just stared at Neil through a crack in my three-ring binder and waited.

When he first saw the note on his chair, he brushed it onto the floor. At first, I was afraid he might just leave it there. But then he leaned over and picked it up.

"Hey! What's this?" he said loudly. Neil is what you'd call a bigmouth. I don't mean he's just loud, either. I mean his mouth is actually big.

He read the note. "Whoa!" he exclaimed. Then he turned around and began raising his eyebrows up and down at me. I think he was trying to get my attention. But I didn't come out from behind my binder.

Neil couldn't keep the news to himself for a second. Quickly, he turned around again and tapped Mona Moore on the shoulder. "Psst! Hey! Get a load of this!"

Neil handed her the note. When Mona finished reading, her eyes were practically bulging out of their sockets. She passed it on to Cory Piper. Then Cory passed it to Mallory Fowler. And Mallory passed it to Matthew Lily. And it just kept going on and on like that, all around the room.

You could hear kids whispering everywhere. Mr. Jolly heard them too. "Hey. What's all the buzzing about?" he asked, looking up from his desk.

Nobody answered, though. Fourth-graders almost never tell what all the buzzing's about.

When the note finally got to Judith Topper, she spun around so fast it made me dizzy.

"*You* wrote this, Rosie Swanson," she hissed. "I *know* you did."

Casually, I sat up in my chair and tossed my hair back. I glanced at the note in her hand.

"Wrote what?" I said, cooler than anything.

She threw it on my desk. "This! You wrote this big, fat lie about Alan Allen!"

Calmly, I smoothed the paper out in front of me and pretended to read. By now a few others had turned around and were watching.

Finally, I looked up from the note and rolled my eyes. "Give me a break, Judith," I said. "Does it look like I wrote this? Have I ever in my life dotted my *i*'s with stupid little hearts?"

Judith's face turned red as a beet. "Liar liar, pants on fire," she hissed again. Then she started doing the "for shame" sign. That's the one where you brush your pointer finger over your other pointer finger.

I didn't let it bother me, though. I just gave her the "cuckoo" sign. That's the one where you twirl your finger in a circle at your head and then point at the person who's cuckoo.

"MR. JOLLY?"

The voice came from the loudspeaker on the wall. It belonged to Mrs. Trumbull, the grouchy school secretary.

Mr. Jolly looked up from his attendance book. "Yes?"

"MR. JOLLY, COULD YOU PLEASE SEND . . ."

Mrs. Trumbull paused. She does this on purpose. Whenever she calls for someone to be sent to the office, she pauses a moment just to make everyone sweat.

". . . ROSIE SWANSON TO THE OFFICE."

Whaaaat? No! It couldn't be!

Mr. Jolly looked back at me. "Rosie?"

Oh God! It was!

"To the office, please," he said lightly.

Everybody turned around to look. Neil McNutt began raising his eyebrows up and down again. Judith Topper clapped.

I tried my best to act unconcerned. I even shrugged my shoulders and forced myself to smile. "Probably just a candidates' meeting or something," I muttered as I stood. My mouth was so dry my lips stuck together.

I still don't remember walking to the office that morning. All I know is that when I finally got there, Mrs. Trumbull was sitting behind her desk looking especially grouchy.

She squinted at me. "Rosie Swanson?"

As soon as I nodded, she pointed her bony finger to Mr. Shivers' office. "Go on in."

I stood there for a second trying to get up

my nerve. Then I took a few steps and peeked around the corner of his door.

I've never been so relieved in all my life. Summer Lynne Jones and Alan Allen were sitting across from Mr. Shivers' desk. It really *was* a candidates' meeting.

I walked through the door and greeted everyone. "Hi, Mr. Shivers. Hi, Summer. Hi, Alan. Hi, Max—"

"Max?" I repeated, confused.

Maxie did not look happy. His arms were folded tightly over his chest, and his cheeks were all sucked into his face. Normally, I would have sat down next to him, but with his face sucked in like that, he wasn't really that attractive.

Just then there was a loud disturbance in the outer office. Mrs. Trumbull was raising her voice. "Put that phone down, young man. Put it down *now*. You are *not* having a stroke."

I heard mumbling. Then Mrs. Trumbull got up from her desk. "Well, I'm sorry, but there's no reason that coming down here should make your legs weak."

More mumbling.

"No. I do *not* have an oxygen tank," she snapped.

The next thing we knew, Mrs. Trumbull was leading Earl Wilber through the door. No one falls apart at the principal's office worse than Earl Wilber. He was pale and drippy and sick-looking.

At first I was more mixed up than before. But then all of a sudden, it made sense. Since Maxie and Earl were a big part of my campaign, they had been invited to the meeting too.

Earl calmed down when he saw the rest of us. "Oh. Whew. Good," he said, wiping his forehead. Then he slipped into the chair between Maxie and me and started taking deep breaths.

Except for Earl's nose whistling, the room was very quiet. Mr. Shivers leaned back in his chair and folded his arms. Then he just stared. He stared for a long time, too. Until we all started to squirm.

Finally, he sat up and narrowed his eyes. Then he pulled a small yellow paper from his top drawer and unfolded it on the desk in front of him.

My stomach cramped up at the sight of it.

Mr. Shivers cleared his throat and began to read:

"Dear Fourth-Grade Friend,

Alan Allen stole a soccer ball from Mort's Sports. Is this the kind of person you want to elect for President of the Fourth Grade?

> Sincerely yours,
> The Committee Who Wants
> You to Be a Good Voter
> and Not Just Vote for the
> Kid Who is the Most Popular"

When he finished, he leaned back and began to stare again.

My heart was pounding like a big bass drum. It was even pounding in my throat. I covered it up with my hand so no one could see.

Another minute went by. I sneaked a peek over at Maxie. He gave me the meanest look I had ever seen. I'm not kidding, either. It looked like he had a skeleton face.

Suddenly, Alan Allen exploded out of his chair.

"Them! It was them!" he blurted. Then he ran over and stood right in front of Maxie and Earl and me. He pointed his finger at each of us.

"Him, him, and her! These three! Right

here, Mr. Shivers! They were the ones who wrote it! I told Zuckerman about the ball, and he told Swanson, and then all three of them got together and wrote that note!"

Maxie jumped up and put his hands on his hips. "No I didn't! I did not! I've never seen that stupid note in my life!"

"You big liar!" shrieked Alan.

Maxie did his skeleton face again.

Earl covered his head with his arms. "Oh geez, oh geez," he whined.

Alan's finger was still in my face. "Get your smelly hand away from me, Alan. I mean it. Get it out now!"

"Oh geez, oh geez, oh—"

"ENOUGH!" Mr. Shivers' booming voice filled the room. Everyone shut up. Even Earl's nose stopped whistling.

The principal stood up, walked around his desk, and sat Alan Allen back in his chair. Then he stood in front of us for a minute—mostly to show us how big he was, I think—and finally went back to his seat.

After that, he made his voice so spooky quiet you could hardly hear it. And he spoke slowly, too. So slowly it was creepy. "I . . . don't . . . like . . . screaming," he whispered. "In fact, I *hate* screaming. So we're not going to scream anymore, are we?"

We all shook our heads no.

"Good," he said. "That's good. Then here's what I would like to do. I would like to ask each one of you a very simple question. And I would like you to give me a very simple answer. Just a yes or a no. Okay? Is that all right with everyone?"

We nodded.

"Thank you so very much," he replied dryly.

Then he swiveled his chair around and faced Summer Lynne Jones. "Okay, here's my question, Miss Jones. And as I said, it's very simple. I just want to know if you had anything at all to do with the note that I just read?"

Summer Lynne's hands were folded on her lap like a little angel's. "No sir," she answered sweetly. "I didn't."

I'm serious. It was so sweet it's a wonder a little halo didn't pop up between her ears or something.

Mr. Shivers nodded. "Fine. Thank you."

Maxie was next. "Okay, Mr. Zuckerman. Same question. Did you have anything at all to do with the note that—"

"No!" interrupted Maxie. "I didn't, either! I mean it! I've never seen that note before in my life!"

Mr. Shivers filled his cheeks with air. For a second, I thought he was going to yell again. But instead, he let the air out slowly and turned to Earl.

His expression softened a bit. "How 'bout you, Earl? Do you know anything about that note?"

Earl wiped his face off with the bottom of his T-shirt. His voice cracked when he said "No."

Suddenly, I just couldn't stand it anymore. "I don't understand any of this, Mr. Shivers," I blurted out. "I just don't. Shouldn't you be asking Alan Allen if he stole the soccer ball? Isn't *that* more important than who wrote the note? I mean, if the newspaper prints a story about a bank robber, the police don't go after the reporter who wrote it, do they? They go after the robber."

"I'm not a robber!" Alan yelled, jumping up from his chair again. "Just because I took a soccer ball from Mort's Sports Store doesn't make me a thief! It happened three years ago, Mr. Shivers. I was only in first grade. That's practically a baby! You can't blame a person for something he did when he was a baby! I'm not a thief! I'm just as honest as any-body. This isn't fair! The election is three days away. How am I supposed to explain this to everyone? It's just not fair."

Alan was so upset he was practically crying. It kind of surprised me, if you want to know the truth. I smoothed my skirt and tried not to look at him.

Mr. Shivers stared at me.

"What about you, Rosie?" he asked quietly. "Do you know anything about this note?"

I looked over at the window and then back again. Suddenly, I felt really confused. I just hadn't expected Alan to practically cry, that's all.

I stretched my neck and tried to look at the little paper still spread on his desk. I felt trapped. "Um, well, let's see. . . . That note doesn't happen to have any little hearts on it, does it?" I said as I squirmed.

I pulled at my collar some more. "Generally, I don't dot my *i*'s with hearts, you know."

Mr. Shivers sucked in his cheeks just like Maxie. "Yes or no, Rosie?"

I looked out the window again. Then I swallowed hard. What was I so nervous about? Alan had admitted that he stole the ball, hadn't he? All I'd done was tell the truth. There's nothing wrong with telling the truth. **105**

The truth is what you're *supposed* to tell. Everybody knows that. Everybody.

I leaned down and pretended to dust off my shoes. While I was down there I nodded yes.

It was all over the board when I came in from lunch recess.

ROSIE SWANSON IS A SNITCH.

ROSIE SWANSON IS A SNITCH.

The news spread like wildfire.

The Second Tuesday in November

☆

Maxie and Earl didn't wait for me after school. I walked home by myself. On the way, three of Alan Allen's friends rode past me on their bikes and shouted, "Yo, snitch! Hi, snitch! How ya doin', snitchy snitch?"

I blinked back the tears in my eyes. Then I cupped my hands around my mouth. "I know you are, but what am I?"

The boys circled back and began to mimic me. "I know you are, but what am I? I know you are, but what am I?" they yelled in high, screechy voices that didn't sound like me at all.

I stuck out my tongue. Sometimes your tongue is all you have left.

Face it, Rosie, I told myself. *You're done for.*

I closed my eyes and tried to picture myself with my bullhorn and golden crown. But all I saw was black.

After the boys rode off, I ran the rest of the way home. I wanted my mother. I don't mean I was going to go bawling to her or anything. But sometimes just being home and *seeing* her there can make me feel a little bit better. Safer, I guess you'd say.

I ran into the house and slammed the door behind me. "Mom?" I called. "Mom? Are you home?"

"Hello, sweetie," a voice answered. It wasn't my mother's voice, though. It belonged to my baby-sitter, Mrs. Rosen from next door. That's exactly what she calls herself too. *Mrs. Rosen from next door.* I used to think it was her name.

"It's Mrs. Rosen from next door," she yelled from the kitchen. "I'm in the kitchen! How 'bout some Oreo cookies and milk?"

That's mostly what Mrs. Rosen from next door does when she baby-sits. She sits in the kitchen, watches our little black-and-white TV set, and eats Oreo cookies.

I like Mrs. Rosen from next door. But seeing her doesn't make me feel better about things. And besides, when the whole world hates your guts, it takes more than milk and cookies to make it better.

I almost started to cry again, but instead, I ran straight upstairs and called Maxie. I knew he was mad about what I had done and all. But still, he was my friend. And friends are supposed to understand you even better than your mother. I heard that on Oprah.

Mrs. Zuckerman answered the phone. "For you, Max!" she shouted when I told her who was calling. He must have asked who it was, 'cause his mother screamed, "ROSIE!" right in my ear.

After that I waited and waited, but Maxie never said "Hello." I held on a long time, too. I thought I heard him breathing once. But when I said his name, he didn't answer.

"Maxie?" I repeated.

Then I heard a click. Then the dial tone.

That's when I finally started to cry.

The next morning, when I got to Maxie's house, Earl was sitting on the steps. Maxie was nowhere to be seen. I figured he was so mad he had decided to walk to school without me.

"Hi, Earl," I said as I walked up.

Earl looked at me and then lowered his head. " 'lo," he mumbled unenthusiastically. I knew he was still upset about his trip to the office, but at least he had waited for me.

I stood there for a minute, but Earl just kept staring at his shoes. Then he untied them, tied them, and untied them again.

I looked at my watch. "Don't you think we'd better go?" I asked at last.

Earl shook his head. "Can't. I'm waitin' for—"

He pointed his finger behind him. I glanced up. Maxie was standing in his doorway glaring down at me. When he finally opened it, he walked straight down the stairs and kept on going. He didn't say a word to me. Not one word.

Earl jumped up and followed him. His shoes were still untied.

I just watched them go.

At first it almost made me cry again. But after a few seconds, I started to get mad. What was wrong with them, anyway? *I* was the one who was in trouble at school, not *them*.

"Hey!" I shouted. "Hey! Why are you guys acting like this? You're not being very good friends, you know!"

Maxie stopped dead in his tracks and threw his head back. "HA!" he bellowed. "THAT'S A GOOD ONE! HA!"

Then angrily, he whispered something to
Earl.

Earl turned around and cleared his throat. "Maxie says that *you're* the one who doesn't know anything about friendship."

I put my hands on my hips. "Oh really? Well, exactly what did I do that was so wrong? I told the truth, that's all! Alan Allen even admitted it, remember? And anyway, *I'm* the one who everybody hates, not you guys!"

Maxie did another loud "HA!" and whispered something else.

Earl turned to face me again. "Maxie says if *you're* the one they hate, then why did *we* get hit with water balloons on our way home from school yesterday?"

Maxie couldn't hold it in anymore. "Yeah! And ask her who crank-called my house last night and wanted to know if Blabber Butt was home. Go ahead, Earl. Ask her that one!"

Earl pivoted. "Maxie would also like to know who called his house last night and asked if bla—"

He tried to say it, but he started to laugh. Maxie gave him a shove. "It's not funny, Earl. I told her all that stuff about Alan Allen and the soccer ball *in confidence*! Ask her if she knows what *in confidence* means. Because for her information, *in confidence* means that you trust somebody not to tell."

Maxie turned and glared at me. "You had no right to do that, Rosie! I get picked on enough as it is. And by the way, in case you haven't figured it out yet . . . you also screwed up your whole election. Who's going to vote for you now? Who the heck is going to vote for a *snitch*?"

The way he said "snitch" made me feel sort of dirty. Like I was a criminal or something.

This time, I couldn't hold back the tears.

Earl saw what was happening. He watched for a second, then came back to where I was standing and ripped off a piece of his book cover. He gave it to me to dry my eyes.

Finally, I started to walk. Earl walked beside me. Maxie waited for us, and we continued on to school in silence.

When we got there, the bell was already ringing. I reached for the door. Maxie put his hand on my arm and gave me a little squeeze.

I practically started to cry again. "I'm sorry, Max. I'm really sorry. I didn't mean to get you in trouble. All I did was—"

Maxie interrupted. "Yeah, I know, Rosie," he said. "All you did was tell the truth."

On the morning of the election, the candidates gathered in Mrs. Munson's room before the assembly. Everybody looked really nervous. We were supposed to be reading over our speeches and stuff, but mostly all we could do was fidget around.

Alan Allen asked Mrs. Munson if he could give the first president's speech. Summer Lynne Jones asked to go last.

I asked to go home.

Mrs. Munson said no.

Finally, we all marched into the media center together. Just like before, the candidates for president were the last to speak. It seemed to take forever to get to us. But when Alan Allen's turn finally came, he stood up slowly and waited for everyone to get totally quiet. Then he walked to the microphone and began.

"My name is Alan Allen," he said. "And I'm running for president of the fourth grade.

"Most of you already know me. I've gone to this school since kindergarten, so I think you know what kind of person I am. I guess if I had to describe myself, I'd say that I'm a good soccer player. And I'd say that I'm honest, too. I don't care what you've heard, either. 'Cause I am.

"I mean, I know there's a rumor going around about how I stole a soccer ball and 113 all. And I'm not saying it's a lie. Only what you probably don't know is that it happened in first grade. When I was six years old. Practically a baby. And even though *certain* people might not understand this, I did lots of stuff when I was a baby that I wouldn't do now.

"Like my mother says I used to scream in restaurants and rub crackers in my hair and junk. And one time I unrolled the toilet paper all over the house. Oh yeah, and this other time when I was in the grocery store, I opened a box of animal crackers, ate a lion, and then put the box back on the shelf.

"But that doesn't mean I'd do it now. 'Cause that would be stupid. Just like stealing is stupid.

"And so I guess I'd just like to say that if you elect me president of the fourth grade, I promise not to do anything stupid. And I'll be fair. And I'll be honest. And oh yeah . . . I won't unroll the toilet paper all over the school. 'Cause even though *certain* people don't understand this, I'm not six years old anymore."

There was lots of clapping. It wasn't very loud, but it lasted a pretty long time. Long enough for Alan to do two extra bows, anyway.

By then, my knees were knocking together like crazy. I still don't know how I made it to the microphone. But somehow I did.

Then I took a deep breath and started my speech.

"Hi. My name is Rosie Swanson. And I'm not one of the popular kids or anything. Mostly I'm just regular. But see, I sort of think that's what makes me special. 'Cause you almost never see regular kids running for office.

"And anyway, being average doesn't mean you're stupid or anything. I have a lot of neat ideas about how to make the school better for us. Mostly they're about lunches. Like I have a plan about how we can organize a committee to go talk to Mrs. Gum, the head cafeteria lady. And how we can sign petitions to get her to stop serving certain gooshy gunk and squishy stuff and that kind of meat with the goopy glop on top.

"I've had the petition idea for a long time. But I didn't say anything 'cause I was afraid it would be stolen. That's one thing I've learned about politics. If you have a really good idea, it's okay for somebody else to "borrow" it.

"There's something else I think I need to talk about too. It's about what happened with

Alan Allen and the notes and stuff. I mean, I'm sure all you guys have heard about it by now. And you probably think I'm a big tattletale or something.

"But see, my grandfather was a police detective. And he's taught me a lot about obeying the law and jail and stuff. And I just think that if you run for president of the fourth grade, you should be honester than almost anybody.

"And I know that when Alan Allen stole the soccer ball he was only six and all. And he probably won't ever steal another soccer ball in his whole entire life.

"But see, that's not really being honester than anybody. 'Cause I wouldn't have even stolen it *then*. Not even when I was *six*.

"And so I guess that's all I have to say . . . except that if you vote for me, I'll try hard to be the best, most honest fourth-grade president you ever saw. And I'll try really hard to get us better lunches, too. I mean it. I will."

A lot of kids clapped. It sort of surprised me, but they clapped me all the way back to my seat.

Something else surprised me, too. When I turned around to bow, Summer Lynne Jones was already standing at the microphone. She didn't look nervous, either. Not one little bit. Mostly she just looked in a hurry to begin.

The clapping had hardly even stopped when she started. It was the shortest speech of the day.

"Hi," she said. "My name is Summer Lynne Jones."

Then she paused real dramatically and waited awhile. You know, like they do in the movies sometimes. And when the room was real quiet—so quiet you could hear a pin drop—she leaned into the microphone again.

"I've never stolen anything in my life.

"And I'm not a snitch."

Slowly, Summer Lynne looked all around the room.

"Think about it," she said solemnly.

Then she sat down.

By the end of the day, Summer Lynne Jones was president of the fourth grade.

Some Stuff I've
Learned . . .

☆

I'm still not exactly sure what happened that day. I mean, I know Summer Lynne Jones got the most votes and all. But I'm not really positive it's because everybody thought she would make the best president. After what happened with Alan and me, I just don't think the voters had much choice.

Nic and Vic Timmerman lost too. So did Roxanne Handleman and Louise the Disease. I saw Louise in the girls' room after school. She was blowing her nose on a paper towel.

Maxie wasn't very sympathetic about my loss. "You did it to yourself, you know," he told me. "You screwed up your whole campaign by writing those notes. And now we'll be getting picked on forever."

"Yeah, well, I don't care," I lied. "It's not the end of the world or anything. I mean, we're not any worse off than we were before, are we? You're still smart, right? And Earl can still draw. And I'm still . . . well, I'm still . . ."

"Nearsighted," offered Earl pleasantly.

I hit him, but it still made me laugh a little bit.

Maxie shook his head and walked away. He takes defeat very personally. Even when it's someone else's.

The other day, the three of us got twirled around on the swings again. It was those same sixth-grade bullies. I told them that they'd better watch out 'cause Mr. Shivers and I were pals. I said I called him Gus.

"And guess what else?" I said. "Just in case you don't know it, I ran for president of the entire fourth grade."

Then the one in the baggy pants took a step backward and said, "Whoa, I'm impressed! Aren't you, Frankie? Aren't you impressed?"

After that, they twirled me twice as fast as they twirled Maxie and Earl. That's the trouble with our society. Politicians don't get any respect at all.

I got twenty-two votes. Judith Topper told me. She overheard Mrs. Munson talking about it in the office. Alan got thirty.

"Twenty-two votes was the worst," said Judith. "I guess you know what that makes you. That makes you the big loser . . . L-O-O-S-E-R."

The girl can't spell worth spit.

The stupid thing is, I think twenty-two votes is pretty good. I mean, after everything that happened, I still convinced twenty-one people (besides myself) that I would make the best president.

I'm pretty sure that Norman Beeman was one of them. He came up to me after school and watched me while I buttoned my sweater. Then all of a sudden, he swooped his hat off his head and covered his heart with it.

"My sincere condolences," he said solemnly. Condolences are sort of like heartaches or something.

I said, "Thank you." It was nice, but Norman still scares me a little.

Another nice thing happened too. The next day, when I was on the playground, two girls from Mrs. Munson's class came up to me and said, "Too bad you lost. We were going to vote for you before that snitch thing."

I'm not sure that they *meant* it to be nice, but it still made me feel good. 'Cause if *they* were going to vote for me, then maybe a lot of other kids were going to vote for me too.

And so this is what I'm thinking. I'm thinking that maybe one of these days I might try running for office all over again. 'Cause my grandfather says that when life gives you a kick in the pants, you're supposed to pick yourself up, dust yourself off, and kick it right back.

And anyway, I think I've learned some stuff about being a better candidate. I mean, I know I'd do better the next time. I even made a list of things to remember about politics. I call it:

Some Stuff I've Learned about Running for Office

1. Think of the best campaign ideas you can. If they're not any good, see what your opponents have come up with. (Stealing is okay in this case.)

2. Be nice to people who make you puke—but not nice enough to make you ashamed of yourself.

3. Smile till your cheeks ache. (Being insincere is also okay.)

4. If you wear glasses, take them off once in a while.

5. A baby thief is not the same thing as a

regular thief. (But I still wouldn't go around bragging about it.)

6. Honesty is always the best policy, except for sometimes when it's not. (In general, voters don't seem to like a snitch.)

7. Try dotting the *i*'s on your posters with hearts.

8. Give the shortest speech.

9. HOPE THAT THE VOTERS DO THEIR JOB!

I put the list on my mirror. I look at it every day. Last night I had a dream about my bullhorn.

Everybody has dreams, you know.

It's the American way.

Maxie's Words

☆

farkleberry (far' kul ber e)—A shrub or small
    tree of the heath family.   [*p. 10*]

dingle (ding' gul)—A narrow valley; glen.   [*p. 28*]

fardel (far' dl)—A bundle; pack; burden.   [*p. 32*]

snool (snool)—One who is meanly
    subservient.   [*p. 71*]